THE CODE

DAVID JUHREN

mlrpress

MLR PRESS AUTHORS

Featuring a roll call of some of the best writers of gay erotica and mysteries today!

M. Jules Aedin	Drewey Wayne Gunn
Maura Anderson	David Juhren
Victor J. Banis	Samantha Kane
Jeanne Barrack	Kiernan Kelly
Laura Baumbach	J.L. Langley
Alex Beecroft	Josh Lanyon
Sarah Black	Clare London
Ally Blue	William Maltese
J.P. Bowie	Gary Martine
Michael Breyette	Z.A. Maxfield
P..A. Brown	Patric Michael
Brenda Bryce	Jet Mykles
Jade Buchanan	Willa Okati
James Buchanan	L. Picaro
Charlie Cochrane	Neil Plakcy
Kirby Crow	Jordan Castillo Price
Dick D.	Luisa Prieto
Ethan Day	Rick R. Reed
Jason Edding	A.M. Riley
Angela Fiddler	George Seaton
Dakota Flint	Jardonn Smith
S.J. Frost	Caro Soles
Kimberly Gardner	JoAnne Soper-Cook
Roland Graeme	Richard Stevenson
Storm Grant	Clare Thompson
Amber Green	Lex Valentine
LB Gregg	Stevie Woods

Check out titles, both available and forthcoming, at
www.mlrpress.com

THE CODE

DAVID JUHREN

mlrpress

Copyright 2010 by David Juhren

Published by
MLR Press, LLC
3052 Gaines Waterport Rd.
Albion, NY 14411

Visit ManLoveRomance Press, LLC on the Internet:
www.mlrpress.com

Editing by Kris Jacen
Cover art by Deana Jamroz
Printed in the United States of America.

ISBN# 978-1-60820-169-3

First Edition 2010

This book is dedicated to all individuals who have ever been forced to deny who they were, while serving their country with courage, pride, and honor.

From the Author

This novel blends historical events and characters with fictional ones. The story of Britain's rush to solve the riddle of the Enigma machine, which was used by the Nazis to put radio messages into code, is a fascinating part of the early years of World War II. The dire plight of England's merchant marine —whose ships were being sunk by the Nazis at enormous cost to England's very survival — and the espionage that took place to solve the Enigma problem, are historical fact.

Virtually all of the characters in this story are fictional, save one. Alan Turing was, in real life, a genius and a homosexual. He spent the greater part of the war years at Bletchley Park, a think-tank whose sole purpose was to decrypt Nazi messages, and he played a major part in breaking Enigma's codes. Some would even say that Turing was *the* one who cracked the Nazis' stricter naval codes, thus saving the merchant marine, and by extension England as well. Many go so far as to assert that if it hadn't been for Alan Turing, England may very well have not won the war at all. But sadly, Turing was arrested in 1952 for charges related to his homosexuality, and he was forced to go through a humiliating "treatment" to "cure" him. What was worse, simply because he was gay, he was stripped of his security clearance — despite having helped win the war against the Nazis, he was actually considered a security risk. Unable to tolerate his treatment by his country's government, Alan Turing took his own life in 1954.

Because I have taken artistic license to some minor facts about the Enigma machine, I suggest the reader, if so inclined, do his or her own research into the fascinating events that led to the cracking of Enigma's codes.

David Juhren

Westchester County, New York

The old man walked along the chalky cliffs of Dover, almost too close to the precipice, but that seemed his style. He walked slowly and carefully though, and when the seagulls that flew around him cried their melancholy scream, it echoed in his soul. He kept to one side of the path, as if he was used to walking this way with someone else.

The loneliness he felt was not new to him, but it had been decades since he'd last felt such pain and emptiness. He reached into his raincoat and pulled out a pack of American cigarettes, lit one and stuck it in the corner of his mouth. The doctor had said he couldn't believe that the old man was in such good health for someone who had smoked all his life. The old man mouthed the first drag, so as not to inhale the sulfur from the match; but the second was smooth, and flowed into his lungs like liquid. He sat on a rock with his thoughts.

February, 1941

Roger dropped the cigarette and stomped it out with his loafer. Seconds later, another bomb exploded. About a quarter of a mile away, but still in the Whitehall area, he suspected. It rumbled like a giant, so different from thunder—an ominous, man-made sound he knew he would never forget.

The Nazis are really dishing it out to London tonight, he thought, standing on the rooftop of his blacked-out apartment building. The structure, like the others in the neighborhood, had been built in the latter part of the last century, and had at one time been dwellings for more affluent inhabitants. Designed, in fact, to be so posh that when the neighborhood was constructed, the streets were torn up, and re-cobbled in broadly curved promenades. All of the buildings in the neighborhood looked alike; four stories high, with columned facades, white gingerbread latticework, and second story *faux* balconies with French doors. But age had taken its toll on the neighborhood, reducing it from its former elegance to that of middle class. The cobblestones had been paved over, yet the water-stained buildings were still architecturally superb, and retained their distinct beauty, like older women who have kept their attractiveness despite unflattering sags and bulges.

The U.S. Embassy had given strict orders that all personnel were to either report to the embassy itself or follow the Londoners down into the Underground. Roger, however, was known by most of his friends to take unnecessary chances with his life, all twenty-eight years of it, as if death might bring some kind of release, and tonight would be no exception. Roger was a political attaché at the U.S. Embassy. His father had worked for the State Department, too, during the Great War, but the elder Mathews had been stationed in Paris. It was through his father's contacts in Washington that he had landed his job—he and his father preferring an ocean between them. Now, the embassy was doing its best to secretly help the English in its war with

Nazi Germany. Despite the fact that the United States would prefer not to enter the war anytime soon, any one of a number of clandestine activities the Americans were doing to assist the British could easily and quickly drag the U.S. into the melee.

Roger had graduated from Georgetown University's School of Government—*summa cum laude*, no less. This was unsurprising, but not because Roger was brilliant. No, it was more because Roger applied himself, for he knew that applying oneself can be more beneficial than possessing an attribute like genius. For three years after college he ran one of his maternal grandfather's factories back in Massachusetts, close enough to his hometown of Boston to visit regularly, which he liked, having spent most of his childhood there. His grandfather had passed away a few years earlier and left his business to Roger's mother and father. Although Roger didn't want to help with the business, he'd acquiesced for the sake of his mother, whom he adored. It had been hell for the first year and a half, until he fell in love. But that situation soured after little more than a year. So, after roughly three years and the end of a relationship, he decided it was time to move on, and begged his father to get him something in Washington. Though on doing so, Roger's father insisted that, if he were to land Roger a job, there would be none of his college shenanigans or "disgusting behaviors."

A flash lit his handsome face, followed a millisecond later by the anticipated explosion. That one was only a few hundred yards away, but Roger stood firm, thinking. He thought of his mother, recalling that last year before she finally succumbed to tuberculosis; it was also the year before he graduated from college. Thoughts emerged of his friends, Stephen from college and John from his family's factory, both of whom he had continued to see regularly, regardless of his father's insistence that he not. To the world, Roger appeared an eligible bachelor, and well educated. Handsome, with his mother's brown hair, and his father's crystal blue eyes, he had small, perfectly shaped ears, a jaw that was slightly dimpled, and lips thin and aristocratic. He was certainly what the English girls called a 'looker,' but he was not complete, nor was he looking for what the English girls offered.

"Why don't you come up and visit me at my family's summer home in Boothbay Harbor?" Stephen asked, his head lying in Roger's lap. They were at their favorite hiding spot on Roosevelt Island, which had only recently been renamed in honor of Teddy. Their favorite tree, a large black oak, shaded them from the sun as they watched the muddy waters of the Potomac roll along. Graduation ceremonies had taken place only the day before, and Washington was seeing its usual summer exodus of congressmen, lobbyists, and students. "You wouldn't have to put up with your father. And now that your mother's gone…" Stephen stopped, realizing he was treading in painful territory for Roger.

"I need to stay in Boston," countered Roger, "so that I can continue getting ready to take over part of my grandfather's business." He was lying. The reason that he wouldn't visit Stephen was because his father had found out about their "friendship," and threatened to disown Roger if he were to continue seeing him. He hated lying to Stephen, but he hated his father more. As if somehow knowing that Roger was lying to him, Stephen replied, "You really need to learn to trust and let go, Roger. In leaps of faith, the hand that catches you will not be seen until after your feet have left the precipice." It was no wonder Stephen graduated in the top three percent of the class, Roger thought, and lowered his head to kiss Stephen. He was always surprised at how exhilarating it was when he kissed a boy. In the distance, a boat somewhere in the Potomac's haze blew its whistle in celebration…

The whistle slowly turned into an air raid siren, which lured Roger out of his slumber. He must have fallen asleep, his head resting against an ancient chimney. The siren marked the end of that night's bombing. He looked at his watch, 4:20 a.m. The sliver of moon had shifted position, surrounded now by a halo of long clouds that glowed a pearly gray.

He stood, stretched, and groggily headed down to his flat. He lived rather well, mostly because on top of his income from the good old U.S. government, he received, much to his father's chagrin, an expense entitlement. It was something that his mother had arranged before she died. He came from money on both sides, and his mother had made sure she personally managed much of what she had brought to the family coffers when she married his father. Roger had lived a very entitled life, but his mother had taught him the value of all people, to be socially responsible to those less fortunate, and to be fair and honest — all of which were hard to do with a father who was filled with anger and cruelty.

His father had grown up in Philadelphia, girdled in a wealthy family with nine other children. He was the fifth child, born to a house and a father who ruled with an iron hand. His mother was an apathetic woman whose main concern was a social life that kept her busy with grand teas, courtly balls, and elegant dinner parties. Neither the oldest nor the youngest, Roger's father was a forgotten child—even the two nannies ignored him. Except by the father's explosive temper—which was usually directed at the children as a group—he was pretty much disregarded.

But there had been a sister, Judith, two years older than Roger's father, who had taken the neglected child into her care. It happened when the two were six and eight years old, and he reveled in the attention. He grew to adore this older sister who loved him, watched out for him, and sheltered him from their father's tirades. She gave him the attention he had always craved, so he was devastated and lost when she died at the tender age of twelve after falling from a tree she'd been climbing.

When Roger was old enough to understand, his mother recounted his father's history, explaining that this was why his father acted the way he did, and although it gave Roger a degree of pity for his father, it didn't really detract from his feeling of resentfulness. At times, in fact, it made Roger, an only child, angrier that his father had grown up with such distant and angry parents, and yet was not empathetic enough to be a compassionate, loving parent himself.

As he entered the apartment he flicked on the lights, which he had remembered to turn off at the beginning of the air raid. Only once had he forgotten to turn the lights out during a raid, and had gotten into a lot of trouble with the street's air-raid warden. A lone, lighted window could be seen by the Luftwaffe's pilots at great heights and used as a target, but worse, if many windows were lighted, the pilots could get a better sense of where they were over London, and hit more strategic targets. So it was imperative that everyone block their windows or turn off their lights during a raid.

He flicked on the walnut-encased radio. The station it was set to was in the middle of playing a popular tune by Vera Lynn called "The White Cliffs of Dover." He sang along with her, and thought about the song's positive outlook on the war. How it looked towards a better tomorrow, when the world was free. *How optimistic the English are*, Roger thought to himself. It was all over the papers how dire their situation was, and yet, in the face of the nightly blitzes and the ongoing war against Hitler, the common person on the street still walked around whistling, the women did their gossiping and laughing, and handsome young men in uniforms walked around joking with their mates.

Roger walked through his spacious living room, maneuvering his way through the large sofa, table, and love seat ensemble that sat in the middle of the room. He picked up and glanced at the previous day's London Times, which rested on one of the two overstuffed chairs in front of the fireplace, then neatly folded it and placed it on his round Chippendale table.

He walked to a small table with a vase-like lamp and flicked it on, further illuminating the walls, tastefully papered with a muted beige pattern. The light from this lamp gave the room a warm, yellowish glow regardless of the time of day or night, and Roger had always appreciated its beauty. On the wall full of shelves, his eye fell on an oval framed photograph of his mother, who had been taken from him far too early. He loved this photo, and believed it to be the only one to fully reflect his mother's beauty. It was nestled among the many books and other photos of his family and friends that populated the bookcase. He picked up an empty water glass he had left on the bookcase the night before and headed into the small kitchenette with its long counter and glass-paned cabinets, which always reminded him of the ones at his family's summerhouse on Cape Cod. He had considered using tape on the cabinets at one point—no sense in having that much glass flying around if a bomb exploded nearby—but he decided they looked too nice to tape up.

He placed the glass in the empty sink, and passed through the small door at the back of the kitchen that led to his den. The den had once been a servant's quarter, but now housed more of Roger's books and photographs. Roger pushed the chair further under the desk that sat against the wall, walked over to the den's large, overstuffed leather chair, and fluffed the pillow that sat upon it. The den opened into his bedroom. Roger always appreciated the fact that the apartment was a full circle. If one went the other way, starting once again from the sitting room, they would enter a short hallway that started from the living room, and ran the length of the apartment. The first door led to the water closet, one of Roger's favorite rooms because he loved its oversized bathtub, which took an impressive twenty minutes to fill. Then down to the end, where again one entered the second door into his bedroom.

Roger opened the door from the den into the bedroom, its walls painted dark burgundy with moss-green accents; the effect one of refined and gentlemanly taste. He picked up the unused pajama bottoms from the night before, which were draped over the chair by the door, and tossed them into the closet, from which he pulled a gray flannel suit, a shirt, and a matching tie. He gently placed these on the huge, thick sleigh bed that had been left by the previous tenant—probably because it was impossible to get through the doors, and God only knew how they had gotten it through in the first place. He had bought the bed's thick, tartan blankets on a trip to Scotland shortly after coming to England. It was a handsome apartment, which those few who had ever seen it called charming. A cleaning woman came twice a week, but Roger usually kept the place neat and organized.

He gave himself a quick wash, got dressed, and was out by the time the sun was peaking over the skyline. Because of the smoke and dust that was hurled into the air, the sunrises over London were beautiful after air raids, and this morning's sunrise was spectacular, with orange and violet drifts of clouds. The only mar was when he turned to the opposite direction of the sunrise, where a number of small ominous columns of smoke rose into the sky. Nevertheless, Roger thought, it looked as if, once the dust and ash settled a bit, it was going to be a crisp and sunny February day.

His morning routine was uninterrupted. He bought his London Times from the boy at the corner and didn't have to wait long for a passing cab to pick him up. He began reading the newspaper, spreading it out over the roomy back seat of the cab. The headline announced that England's supply line was drastically in peril due to the Nazis' constant sinking of Britain's merchant ships, which took down with them their precious cargo.

Because of the fires raging in White Hall from the previous night's bombing, his cab ride to the embassy at Grosvenor Square took longer than usual. Roger didn't mind, though, because it afforded him the chance to read more of the morning's paper. The eastern sky was bright, almost sunny, as he paid the driver and jumped out of the cab. As it drove away, he turned to look up at the heavy, yet delicately ornate exterior of the Annex, which the English had given the Americans shortly after the start of the war. It was called the Annex because it sat away from the rest of the Embassy's compound at the Court of St. James and having been built originally as a bank, contained fortified walls, strongholds, and vaults that made for safe places during air raids. It reminded Roger of Washington's National Archives Building, upon whose steps he'd sometimes sat and read, and where he gained an appreciation of that structure's resonating sense of protection and security. The Annex now gave him the same feeling, and he liked it. Nodding to the marines at the gate and flashing his identification tag, Roger walked up the twenty-three stone steps (he had counted them many times) that ran the length of the building, and entered the marbleized sanctum of the large foyer. He was halfway up the grand marble stairway when he heard his name being called.

"Mr. Mathews!" the voice of the young woman softly echoed from the walls of the foyer. It was Judith Feniway, secretary to the Embassy's Chief of Staff. He had known Judy since long before the war, their parents having been acquaintances back in Boston, and so Roger had met her at a number of social events of Boston's elite. He waited on the landing for her to climb the polished stairs and catch up with him.

"Judy, good morning," he said, smiling genuinely as she walked up the last three stairs. "Glad to see you've survived another one of Hitler's attacks."

"Barely," pushing a lock of blond hair behind her ear. "The building right across the street from mine took a direct hit, and killed a family of six. I had become friends with the eldest daughter and had spoken to her on a number of occasions. It's just so tragic, Roger. I don't know why they hadn't gone to the Underground."

"Judy, I'm sorry." Roger was clearly concerned.

"I wish they'd hurry up and end this thing," she whispered as they started climbing the stairs. "Or at least maybe we could enter the war and help the English end it sooner." Their conversation was being underscored by an ambulance's wailing siren in the distance.

"Well, at least we're helping as best we can without getting into the war," Roger said as they stopped at the banister at the top of the stairs. Roger followed Judy's gaze to a shaft of dust-filled sunlight that fell on a fern at the top of the landing. Roger, too, became mesmerized by the sunlight but pulled out of it after a few seconds of silence.

"Are you all right?"

"Yes, I'm fine, thanks, Roger. Chief of Staff Peligro wants you to be in on a meeting this afternoon. It's about the recent work you've been doing, so you might want to bring your files and do your homework," she smiled. "It's at the British Admiralty Building at three thirty, and you'll be riding in the Chief of Staff's car for a pre-meeting briefing at three o'clock." She started back down the stairs.

"Thanks, Judy. I'll be ready," turning and heading toward his office.

Peligro was the embassy's Chief of Staff, and Roger was titillated by being asked to join such a high-ranking meeting. The Admiralty was the nerve center of the English Navy, and anything taking place there was of the utmost importance.

As he walked the maze of corridors and hallways to his office, Roger reviewed the year that had passed since he had arrived at the embassy, and how quickly things had moved along for him. Upon assuming his duties, he'd been immediately put to work with members of His Majesty's Government, along with a few select members of the State Department and U.S. military, to finish an assessment of Germany's use of encryption devices and the various tools the Nazis were using to send and receive coded messages. Working at the very secretive British Cryptanalytic Department at Bletchley Park, he was introduced to Alan Turing, the English mathematical genius working on solving the Enigma machine, which was being used to put the Nazis' secret messages into codes. The Enigma machine had become Alan's life by then, and it soon became Roger's, too.

Their relationship became very close, with Alan adoring Roger, the handsome young American, as Roger was attracted to Alan's genius and impishly youthful looks. It was known amongst certain sets in London that Alan was a homosexual, but Alan didn't care much what others thought of him. Roger, on the other hand, felt the need to be very secretive about how things looked from the outside. Alan obliged Roger's request for secrecy, and their relationship from the outside took the façade of a good working alliance; yet for the three weeks they had been together, they were very much a couple. Roger looked back on that time as one of those relationships hard to place on the continuum between friendship and love. At least on the friendship level, they had, indeed, loved each other very much, and there had also been a lot of physicality, which made it fun and sexually gratifying. As quickly as they had fallen into this loving friendship they fell out of it, but on the best of terms.

It was a healthy changeover, Roger thought as he instinctively stooped to help a secretary pick up some papers she had dropped in the hallway. He smiled as she thanked him, and he continued on towards his office. He marveled that he and Alan continued to have the strongest of friendships—either man would do anything for the other.

As Roger entered his office, he stopped to look around at the books and files that occupied the space he had moved into a year earlier, papers that related the history of the infamous Enigma machine. It was used not only to put messages into secret code, but could also be used to decode messages as well. The Germans had been using the Enigma machine in one form or another for over ten years. It was, in principle, a rather simple device, but one wrought with intense internal complexity, and one whose output was bewildering, to say the least. It contained "rotors" that moved a notch with each character entered and assigned that character its own code letter. Put simply, each of the Enigma's circular rotors had twenty-six characters, and each time a character was assigned a code letter, one of its rotors would turn $1/26^{th}$ of a notch before assigning the next code letter. The result of this was that, even if the letter "a" appeared twice in the same word, neither "a" would have the same corresponding code letter.

The English didn't have the time or resources it would take to try each possible permutation of the code. But neither had Poland in the years leading up to the war, and yet they had discovered a way to break the Nazis' earlier codes. What the Poles found useful was a mathematical system called permutation theory which reduced this time to a more realistic schedule. Poland's move to break the code had come in response to a little-known man named Adolph Hitler, who had just been elected to office, but who in 1933 quickly seized control of the German government and began pushing his military leaders to develop treaty-breaking militaristic might. As the thirties wore on, the *Reichstag* began making menacing threats to the Polish government.

In 1939 the Poles, using decoded messages, knew they were about to be invaded by the Nazis, and arranged a secret meeting with British Intelligence. They surprised the British by handing over all of the Enigma equipment and information they possessed. In turning over its knowledge of the Enigma machine, Poland gave the English a greatly needed head start. No one knew it at the time, but the Nazis, with the addition of three new rotors, had just vastly improved the Enigma machine. This would bring the number of rotors to five, rendering the Enigma's codes almost unbreakable.

Since then, the English had been urgently trying to break the codes. On top of almost daily blitzes from the Luftwaffe, the German Navy was torpedoing Britain's merchant ships at a perilous rate. England's plight was desperate, and it would be only a matter of months before it would run out of supplies. That's what was driving the deciphering efforts at Bletchley Park, and what was motivating this group of Englishmen and Americans through every waking hour.

Roger thought about his admiration for Alan, who was more than a mathematician, he was a philosopher—a combination that made him a fascinating person to be around. Roger loved to listen to Alan's lengthy dissertations about the world, his thoughts on life and death and the internal mechanisms of the universe. Alan would go into lengthy discourses about the future and the wondrous things it would bring. Like machines that would eventually think and perform computations and tasks at speeds not unlike those of the human brain.

But these other interests were now secondary, and Alan, who had already done major work on cracking the Enigma's previous codes, was currently working on a more formidable problem. Bletchley Park had recently turned its attention to the German Navy's development of a stricter Enigma code that was proving almost impossible to break. It was this new coding method that was causing the British to steer their merchant ships straight into the paths of waiting German U-boats. If this new code wasn't broken soon, England could well lose the war. Without England to worry about, the Nazis would easily conquer the rest of Europe, including the Soviet Union, and become the largest and most powerful nation on the planet. Alan was heading a team that was close to breaking the German Navy's stricter encoding methods, but the final key was proving elusive and obtuse.

As Roger sat at his desk, his mind quickly turned to what he might need at today's meeting. Being called to join a meeting at the British Admiralty was no small thing. He had labored greatly to get to this point in his life, and always worked harder than most. Maybe it was his own homosexuality, and the internalized struggles caused by a society set against the love of two people of the same sex that drove him—and not by coincidence a drive possessed by other gays Roger knew—to stay one step ahead of his peers.

Getting up, he passed through the very narrow suite he shared with his secretary, Elizabeth. He went past her neat desk, opened a file cabinet and pulled out their master file, then headed back to his own desk, which sat under a very large window. Roger liked a lot of light, and usually kept the shades drawn open, even when the sun splashed blindingly across his desk. This always reminded him of when he was first assigned Elizabeth.

He had already been at the embassy a few days, and was in his office with his back to the door when he heard a raspy voice say, "Your papers are all going to turn yellow with all that sunlight on 'em." It was Elizabeth, with a deep London accent to boot. He swiveled around to see the short, white-haired lady standing at his doorway. He told her he liked things with an historical look, to which she replied that he'd then like having her around, which made them both laugh, and since then they had been good friends. Elizabeth was smart, but more importantly intelligent, and although she had never gone to Oxford, she exhibited a sophisticated view of the world and was able to analyze problems using an amazing knowledge of facts and figures. She was also very faithful to Roger in a maternal way and on occasion had gone out of her way for him. She mothered him, and he treated her as he would have treated his own mother.

He sat down and began a list of what documents he'd need to bring to the afternoon's meeting. It was still early, but already the sound of typewriters and voices could be heard filtering into the hallways. Although working at the embassy was a job, both American and English staffers knew that somewhere at that very moment, there were brave men who were doing the actual fighting and dying in this war. So coming in early and staying late, working at home, and donating their time to war drives was their way of supporting the war effort.

Elizabeth came in wearing her customary brown "uniform," which always reminded Roger of an outfit that would have been worn by a headmistress of a reformatory school. But like most English women working jointly for the U.S. and British governments, she wore her uniform proudly. She went to work without so much as a word, and was in his office in ten minutes, carrying several folders under her left arm.

"Good morning, Mr. Mathews. I trust you slept well?" This was a private joke between the two, as few Londoners slept at all during bombing raids.

"Slept like a baby," he grinned, not removing his eyes from the paper he was writing on. He dotted a period and handed the sheet to Elizabeth.

"Elizabeth, I've been asked to attend a meeting at the Admiralty, and have been told to prepare for it." He raised his face now to look at her and hand her the sheet he'd been writing on. "I'll need the following papers and files before three o'clock."

She took the list with her right hand, examined it, and placed the files she was holding on his desk.

"Here are all of 'em, except the Coding file, which we don't have because it's still with the Department of Navy. I'll have it here by two o'clock." She started to walk out of his office when Roger started to say something, and she cut him off as she continued walking, "I know, I know, I bumped into Ms. Feniway. She told me."

He smiled at the now empty doorway, and went back to his preparations. He was both elated and nervous at having been asked to join this meeting. He couldn't wait to wire his father about it, and only wished he could see the old bastard's face when he read it. Ever since he was a boy, he had succeeded at almost everything he touched and yet nothing was good enough for his father. It wasn't really that his father thought he could do better, only that he thought Roger never really did well enough. But this, this taking part in a meeting at the Admiralty on such a highly significant matter, certainly should impress the old man.

Roger was at the office of the Chief of Staff shortly before three that afternoon. He had met Mr. Peligro several times, and given him a number of briefings on the Enigma machine. He was shown into the large office where Mr. Peligro was seated at his desk. Another man was seated in one of two low, sunken armchairs that were situated across from the desk, both men were silhouetted by large windows that took up half the room and framed by heavy moss-colored curtains.

"Roger, how are you?" Peligro greeted him, rising and shaking Roger's hand from behind his desk. "I'd like you to meet Milton Pomboi of the FBI," he motioned to the middle-aged man who was now moving to a standing position. Roger shook Pomboi's limp hand and looked into the stony face of age-worn arrogance, but also an undeniable intelligence. Pomboi looked older than his age, and his face had many wrinkles caused, Roger assumed, by a lifetime of pure career-mindedness and daily doses of cigarettes and cheap gin.

"Good to meet you," Pomboi said, with so little sincerity that nothing on his face moved but his mouth.

"Let's get going, we'll explain a bit of what's going on in the car," Peligro said putting on his coat.

The ride to the Admiralty Building was not a long one, and the Embassy's Chief of Staff didn't need that much time anyway.

"Roger, we're meeting with the British on something that you will be involved in—Milton, can you explain?"

"Well, Mr. Mathews," Pomboi began, "we can't go into great detail now, but let me just say that the British are in a position where they will do almost anything to break the Enigma codes. I'm sure you saw this morning's London Times?"

"Why, yes," Roger answered, "that if the tonnage of lost supplies because of merchant ships being torpedoed continues at this rate, England has only about seven months before… before…"

"Before it must throw in the towel and negotiate a separate peace," Pomboi finished, his yellowish fingers lighting a cigarette. "I'm glad you understand the gravity of their situation, Mr. Mathews. Keep that in mind when we meet with them in a few minutes." It was then that Roger noticed that Pomboi had a slight accent, but because it was so slight, he couldn't tell what kind of accent, though certainly European.

"Can I ask, sir," Roger said, turning now towards Mr. Peligro, "what my involvement might be in this matter other than supplying information on Enigma?" He was now somewhat bewildered and just barely covering his intimidation by the FBI agent. Pomboi put him on edge, and Roger was trying everything he had not to stammer, or say something stupid.

"You can ask," Peligro responded, "but your answer won't really come until we're in the meeting." Roger nodded and turned to the window, watching the city pass as the car neared the Admiralty Building, looming in the distance, its façade oddly lit in the rare February sunlight.

❖   ❖   ❖

They arrived at the Admiralty and were led to a back meeting room with a large table that could easily seat twenty. Apparently, however, there would only be seven of them—three Americans and four British. Roger was glad to see that one of them was Alan, sitting at the oversized conference table reviewing notes. Alan noticed the American delegation entering, and when his eyes fell on Roger, his face lit up with a smile. Roger smiled back, and mouthed "hello." There was an older gentleman with bushy gray sideburns that matched the size and bushiness of his eyebrows. He wore the uniform of an admiral of the Royal Navy, and he too was sitting at the table looking at a file. Roger couldn't help but also notice a very handsome and well-built young naval officer, a captain by the looks of the uniform and insignia, chatting with a red-haired, middle aged gentleman in a dark, pinstripe suit.

"Good afternoon, gentlemen," the man with the bushy sideburns said, standing up. "Please take a seat, and we can begin. Let me begin by making some introductions, though some of you know most of the people here. I am Admiral James Welles of His Majesty's Navy. To my left is Mr. Robert Simpson of British Intelligence." Welles nodded in the direction of the gentleman with reddish hair. "Next to him is Doctor Alan Turing, one of England's foremost mathematicians. Next to Doctor Turing is Captain Clive Westmore, also of His Majesty's Navy." He motioned to the handsome young naval officer. Roger tried to determine whether the captain was very young looking for his age, or whether he had made that rank earlier than most. Nevertheless, Roger thought he looked no older than himself. "Our American contingent is comprised of the American Embassy's Chief of Staff, Mister Anthony Peligro, Special Agent Milton Pomboi of the FBI, and Mister Roger Mathews, special attaché of the American Embassy."

"Those seated in this chamber," the admiral continued, leaning forward in his chair, "possess the top most security clearance of both American and British governments. As you may tell from those called to this meeting, we are here to discuss a new development in our endeavors to decode Enigma." The admiral opened a file in front of him, and glancing at a paper on top, continued. "As you know, possession of all five rotors of the Enigma machine would give us the complete ability to decode all of Germany's strict naval codes," His thick gray eyebrows moved up and down with each syllable. "His Majesty's Government has been in possession of one of the five Enigma rotors—the second out of the fifth, in fact, otherwise called Rotor II."

Although everyone at the conference table probably already knew this fact, all smiled and nodded in satisfaction, knowing how important possession of *any* of the Enigma's rotors was to solving the problem.

Roger looked over at Alan, who smiled and gave him a wink.

Alan had not only informed Roger of Rotor II, but had actually let Roger see it a few weeks before on a visit to Bletchley Park, where Alan and his team were working feverishly to use it in their models.

"However," Welles continued, "as you know, one rotor does not a full set make, and therefore, despite the ingenious work of Dr. Turing and others, without a complete set of rotors, we are at a standstill." He turned towards Mr. Simpson and gave him a nod to take over.

"Last evening," Mr. Simpson began, "the HMS Gleaner, a minesweeper trolling the Firth of Clyde, came across a Nazi submarine U-33 as it was sowing mines. A few depth charges brought the U-boat to the surface, where the crew had a chance to escape before the submarine sank. Wanting to make sure they made it impossible for us to later acquire the rotors from the sunken U-boat's Enigma machine, they gave two of the sailors the rotors as they left the sinking vessel, with instructions to toss them away from the ship as they emerged, thus scattering them on the ocean floor." Simpson looked up from his paper, and then looked back down. "One of the men wasn't aware of the importance of his instructions, and in the confusion of a sinking submarine, the splashing around in the cold waters of the Firth of Clyde, and the daring rescue by the crew of the Gleaner, he failed to discharge his duties."

"Are you telling us that you have another rotor?" Alan asked.

"No," Admiral Welles piped in. "He's telling you that we now have *three* more rotors." A moment of surprised silence gripped the table, but was immediately followed by a wave of gleeful applause from practically everyone at the table. Roger noticed the stoical Pomboi merely nodding his satisfaction.

"Gentlemen, please!" Simpson said through a smile. After a few seconds the room calmed down, but jubilation still permeated the air. "What's more serendipitous, and quite astonishing at that, is that the rotors confiscated were numbers I, III, and V. Therefore, having already obtained Rotor II, we need only add

Rotor IV to make a complete set, and then fully have the capacity to decode Enigma. I turn the table back to Admiral Welles."

"Thank you," Welles began again. "A few months ago we received an interesting offer from the attachés of the French Resistance. In exchange for a delivery on our part of several tons of ammunition, arms, and surplus, they would give us an Enigma rotor they had confiscated. Further investigation on our part showed that, unless this is a very good forgery, they are, indeed, in possession of a Rotor IV, the very one we now need."

The men around the table were motionless as they listened.

"We told the Resistance contacts that we were uninterested. Back when this offer was made, their rotor would have given us two; however, it was determined at the time that the cost of the barter was too steep. Especially in light of the fact that it would require us to perform a risky operation that involved a clandestine meeting in occupied France where the Enigma rotor would be traded for the surplus. Which leads us to where we are now," Admiral Welles paused a second, looking up to make sure there were no questions.

"The American Embassy and His Majesty's Government have agreed that the French Resistance is to be contacted again, and that we should endeavor to go ahead with their offer," Admiral Welles continued, gesturing with the pen he held in his oversized hand. "This operation will require extreme organization, autonomy, and concentration of effort."

At this, Roger found a large brown envelope being pushed in front of him by Mr. Pomboi, while at the same time a matching envelope was pushed in front of Captain Westmore. Again, Roger noticed how handsome the young captain was. Their eyes met, held each other for a second, and then turned back to Welles.

"Therefore," Admiral Welles continued, "Mister Roger Mathews from the American Embassy and Captain Clive Westmore of the Royal Navy have been selected by their governments to handle this mission. Mr. Mathews is an expert on the many facets of the Enigma machine and its history, and he has worked closely with Dr. Turing at Bletchley Park, who will act as a consultant to this mission." Admiral Welles turned a page in his files. "Captain Westmore has been selected for this mission for his experience in dealing with the French Resistance, as well as a number of occasions working from behind enemy lines in France. Both men will report to me and are expected to move expeditiously in retrieving Rotor IV. I will meet with Mr. Mathews and Captain Westmore after this meeting to brief them on their duties and answer any questions they may have. However, if anyone has a brief question, please ask, but I'll remind you that due to the secrecy of this mission, we'd prefer you keep your question general."

"How long do you envisage this taking?" asked Peligro.

"We are hoping three weeks—four if we run into complications," Admiral Welles answered.

"And decoding the German signals would begin…?"

"Within hours," Admiral Welles replied. "We have our copies of the Enigma machine ready. We're just waiting for the rotors. Any further questions? Good, then if Mr. Mathews and Captain Westmore would be so kind as to remain behind, this meeting is adjourned, and I remind all present that the level of secrecy of all that was heard here is of the utmost importance."

Peligro leaned over to Roger. "I'm sorry, Roger. We couldn't have told you earlier because we were still discussing the plans with the British. However, you were our first choice for the job, and we're confident you'll see the rotor safely back to England."

"Thank you, sir. I will do my best," Roger replied, smiling.

"See that you do," a voice almost whispered low and daring to his left, and Roger turned to see the grim-faced Pomboi looming above him.

Peligro rose and was followed out of the room by Pomboi. Alan followed soon after, motioning to Roger with his hand to call him on the phone, while Mr. Simpson got up and was chatting with Admiral Welles by the door. Roger waited a few seconds and then got up to stretch his legs. He walked to the full-length window and looked out onto the street below, trying to absorb what was said at the meeting, but his mind strayed to a different time and place…

John leaned over, gently brushing a lock of hair that had fallen over Roger's handsome face. It was around nine thirty at night, and they were both working late, pouring over the books for the tax examiner who was expected to arrive the following morning. Roger looked over and smiled at John, who had beautiful brown eyes that contrasted handsomely with his dark blond hair. Their eyes held each other's gaze for a wonderfully full moment, and then John pulled the ledger closer.

"We need to finish this tonight because we won't have time in the morning," he said, flipping the pages of the large, green-leather binder.

"I know," Roger blurted sarcastically. "But I'm so distracted with you around," he added with a grin.

"Roger, you know damn well that if anyone were to suspect anything, I'd be the one out of here on my ass, not you. You are the grandson of the founder of this company, you're practically running this factory on your own, and will be here long after they've expelled me. You, Roger my dear, are indestructible," he laughed. Roger loved when John laughed because his face lit up and his eyes sparkled with a deep sensitivity. Roger leaned over and kissed John, who returned the affection. It was only for a moment, far too short, John whispered his name…

"Roger?" It was not John's New England accent, but an English accent, and Roger felt a gentle hand touch his elbow. He slowly turned to see Captain Westmore standing next to him at the window. He was even more handsome close up, and his naval uniform accentuated his attractiveness. The captain had a slender face with gray blue eyes, dark blond hair that fell low on his forehead, and he carried his trim but strong body with an aristocratic air. Even his accent hinted of an aristocracy that Roger found extremely appealing. Maybe it was the juxtaposition between the captain's athletic frame and his gentleness, but Roger was immediately attracted to him.

While Roger was performing his appraisal, the captain continued to stand with the hint of a smile, head slightly cocked to one side.

"Er, yes, captain," Roger blurted, coming out of his reverie.

"Hello," the captain said, extending a hand that jutted from a spotless white sleeve. "I just want to formally introduce myself, and say that I'm happy we'll be working together on getting Rotor IV."

"Yes, captain, likewise," Roger grinned while slowly taking the extended hand. Their handshake was solid and masculine and, much to Roger's enjoyment, lasted a second longer than it probably should have.

"If we're going to be working together, you must drop the "captain" business. Please call me Clive."

"Then Clive it is," Roger said. He was lost in the moment of standing here talking to this well-built, extremely handsome, articulate man who, like himself, had become quite successful at a young age. And now they were expected to spend a lot of time together working on this covert mission. His mind raced on two engines—an emotional and physical attraction to his new colleague, and his excitement in taking part in this secret mission.

"Mister Mathews, Captain Westmore," Admiral Welles beckoned, sitting at the table in the now-empty room.

The two men grew somewhat serious, and walked back to the conference table. Whereas Roger immediately sat down, Clive remained standing at attention, in deference to his superior.

"At ease, captain," Welles commanded, and Clive took a seat next to Roger.

"Gentlemen," Welles began, "basically everything you need is in the envelopes presented to you at the meeting. I suggest you read it all very carefully, then work together to get this job done. I expect a one-page status report every other day, and a meeting with either or both of you once a week. Captain Westmore, Mr. Mathews, this is a most dangerous mission—dangerous in that the political stakes for the United States are most high, and that exposure could endanger America's ability to continue helping England. It would certainly prove scandalous to President Roosevelt. Do I make myself clear?"

"Yes, sir," both men replied.

"Good," Welles said, rising up from his chair and lumbering towards the door. "Then I'll meet with you at 0800 hours the day after tomorrow. Good day."

Clive spent the rest of the afternoon in Roger's office as they discussed primary plans for the operation. They made telephone calls to subordinates and colleagues, getting information from them in ways that would never impart even the slightest hint of their task at hand. They planned meetings with the London-based representative of the French Underground. They pored over papers, reports, and classified documents.

In the days that followed, between setting the preliminary plans for the mission, they got to know each other better. They talked about their childhoods, the differences and similarities of the British and American governments, how much it meant that America and England were so closely allied for the defeat of Nazi Germany, if only secretly. They also discussed what it was like being young men from privileged families. Apparently, Clive was the second son of an English Lord, and would inherit neither title nor manor, but was at least set for life financially. He was sent to Oxford, was trained in English and French literature, and was about to begin teaching in one of Oxford's colleges, but the war broke out, and he joined the armed forces. Roger was glad that in all their conversations there seemed to be no mention of past or present girlfriends, but he knew it was almost inevitable, as was the case whenever he was attracted to a fellow, that Clive probably had one or two girlfriends stashed here and there. Eventually Clive did say he had dated a young lady when he was in Oxford, but that it didn't work out, and since then, life was far too busy and complex for courtship. Clive listened intently to Roger's stories about growing up in New England and about his grandfather's rise from a Scottish immigrant to a wealthy industrial baron.

One cold and rainy Sunday afternoon in Roger's flat, they found they had one important thing in common—they both got along terribly with their fathers.

"A bastard of a man if there ever was," said Clive. "My father is a pompous ass who acts as if it were he who brought the lordship to the family, rather than my great-great-great grandfather. Sadly, my family hasn't really contributed much to England since then."

"I kind of think it has now," Roger said, gently smiling into Clive's face.

Clive had to think for a second, and then smiled back. "Well, that's if we can get Rotor IV back here in one piece."

For the next two weeks, the men spent most of their time in meetings—meetings with each other, with Admiral Welles, or with members of the French Resistance who possessed the coveted Rotor IV. Jean Pierre Du Mont, the representative of the French Resistance group that possessed the rotor, was a young man in his mid-twenties who had risen in the ranks of the Resistance through a combination of bravery, luck, and charm. He was exquisitely good looking—Gallic dark and thin, with a pencil mustache and gold-specked hazel eyes. They had arranged to meet him at his apartment in Soho, and were now sitting around a small, round table with a cheap green tablecloth tossed over it. Roger noticed that there were small stacks of papers and magazines beneath the tablecloth, and that he had to be careful how he rested his teacup.

"We need the guns, ammunition, and medical supplies delivered to these three towns," the Frenchman said, offering Clive a piece of paper.

"But these places are very far apart from each other. It's already a dangerous enough mission for us without having to extend ourselves this far," Clive replied in perfect French, and Roger remembered Clive mentioning that his mother had been born and raised in Montpellier.

"I understand, but we must have these arms delivered to these locations," Jean Pierre repeated, this time in French, touching the paper that Clive had handed to Roger.

"But what about your communication networks, which we know are top-rate and exceedingly well placed," Roger added, his French not as good as Clive's. "Surely these are avenues you could use to deliver these things yourself, no?" Like a magician's trick, Jean Pierre produced a cigarette from behind his ear, and Clive was quick to offer him the light. The smoke curled up toward the light that hung from the ceiling.

"Messieurs, my friends, these are communication networks only," he said, nodding a thank you to Clive. "It would be impossible for us to deliver this heavy load." It was apparent that the man wasn't going to budge.

The meeting lasted hours, but eventually Clive and Roger were able to talk Du Mont into a number of things. It took them quite a bit of time to agree on the amount of arms and surplus equipment that would be given. Clive did most of the talking on this matter, because they had agreed before the meeting that the amount of supplies would be determined based on the size of the small experimental landing ship that the Royal Navy was lending the mission.

Several months earlier, when France fell, hundreds of thousands of retreating British troops were trapped on the French coast at Dunkirk with the full might of the Nazi war machine closing in, and with no logistical way of rescuing this many men—it was impossible. However, when it was made public that the army was basically lost, an amazing event took place. From the coast of England, and streaming from its tributaries, estuaries, and coastal villages, an armada of every imaginable craft began heading to the coast of France; yachts and fishing boats, skiffs and motorboats, thousands of leisure craft spent days sailing between France and England, rescuing their bleeding and war-torn sons.

The rescue at Dunkirk was a miracle, but England was forced to leave all its military equipment behind, only to be confiscated by the Nazi army. It was then that Prime Minister Churchill ordered the Royal Navy to work with the United States Navy to develop a ship that could easily and quickly transport tanks and equipment. The ship that would carry Clive and the surplus equipment across the channel was one of only three newly constructed and smaller prototypes of this new ship. The ship, called a Landing Ship Tank, or LST for short, could beach itself and its bow could fold down, allowing vehicles to drive on or off.

The plan was for Clive and three trucks loaded with supplies to cross the English Channel and be delivered right to the beach. After the trucks had been driven off, the ship would turn back for England, leaving Clive to fend for himself. Clive alone behind enemy lines gave Roger pause, and he was deeply, if secretly, concerned for Clive's safety. He was quickly becoming enamored of Clive, and the amount of time they had been spending together gave Roger a butterfly-in-the-stomach feeling whenever his new friend knocked at the door, or called on the phone—he was steadily falling in love. Roger had taken to lying in bed at nights, listening to the February rain falling on his window and thinking about he and Clive together. He fantasized about making love with Clive, and dreamt of spending Sunday mornings together laughing and joking in his oversized bathtub. What he longed for most, though, was the long-term emotional attachment and delicate caring that had always eluded him in previous relationships. Yet, Clive seemed to be uninterested, hadn't dropped a single cue, nor had he used any homosexual code words. So, Roger assumed that

Clive was not gay.

The following day was rainy and dreary, and they worked non-stop cooped up in Roger's office reviewing maps, measuring distances between the cities where they were to deliver the surplus, and researching the current placement of Nazi divisions in those cities. They wanted to make sure the convoy of trucks made the widest possible detours around the most heavily concentrated areas of German occupied towns.

It was well past eight o'clock when they decided to call it a night. Neither of the two men had eaten since lunch, and they were starving.

"There's a pub not too far from here that serves up a pretty good brisket, despite the rationing," Roger proffered.

"Great, I can't believe I've gone so long without eating," Clive responded, smiling up at Roger as he put all his papers into his weathered leather bag.

Roger noticed that despite Clive being in a uniform all day, it showed no creases and seemed virtually unwrinkled. Roger wondered if this was due to the material the English used for their uniforms, or whether it was a commentary on Clive's neatness. Roger was glad they were calling it a night because he was having a hard time keeping his mind on the task at hand. He found himself continually daydreaming about Clive. His imagination put them anywhere—naked on the beach of some deserted tropical island, secluded in some Scottish cottage—anywhere there was privacy. Roger was finding it too difficult to pay attention. A few days earlier, and only for a millisecond, he'd thought about leaving the mission because he couldn't keep his mind on things. But how could he explain such an action to his superiors? What would he say? That he was stepping aside because he had fallen in love with this English naval captain? But such a scenario was impossible anyway, and Roger would have to put himself through the agony of having fallen in love with someone who in all likelihood would not return the affection.

At the pub, they gorged themselves, not only on the food, but also on one another, as each continued to learn all he could about the others life, aspirations, hopes, and dreams.

"And what do you want to do after the war?" Clive asked Roger.

"Me? I'm going to head back to Washington, finish what I need to do at the State Department, then go back to Massachusetts and run the family business." Roger hoped this didn't sound too boring a plan, especially after a few exciting years as a diplomat to the Court of Saint James.

"Oh, that sounds wonderful." Clive stretched back in his seat, and crossed his feet. He clasped his hands behind his head, which made his arms bulge with muscle and expanded his shoulders. "What sort of business did you say your family owned? I'm liable to come with you!"

"You are most certainly welcome to join me," Roger tested, cocking his head and smiling in a way he only saved for flirting. "As to the kind of factories we own, well, there are several, actually," Roger explained. "We own about three steel mills and four factories that were making parts for the railroad industry. But my father and I quickly converted two of the factories to making components for airplanes. Ours were some of the first to be shipped to Britain under President Roosevelt's orders, even though Congress said the U.S. couldn't send military equipment to England. But of course, this wasn't military equipment, these were just parts that you guys were putting together into fighter airplanes," Roger finished, both men chuckling.

"Here's to American ingenuity and English logic!" declared Clive, raising his beer mug.

"And," Roger said softly, "may our friendship be as strong and close as our two nations."

"Closer, still, Roger, closer still," Clive quietly agreed. His hand slid along the bench they were sitting on and rested it on Roger's hand. Roger waited a second, then two, then, boosted by three ales, he turned his hand upward, taking Clive's in his own. Their backs to the wall and the hands hidden by the tablecloth, no one could see them holding hands. There were only four other people in the place, and two of them seemed to be asleep at the bar with the other two were lost in quiet conversation with the bartender.

Roger couldn't believe this was happening. Their eyes locked for what seemed eternity. Both sheepishly grinned on realizing they were holding hands, but neither rushed to pull their hand away. After a few seconds, Clive picked up his mug with his free hand and nonchalantly took a sip of beer. It gave Roger the impression that his wasn't the first boy's hand to be held by Clive.

While their hands danced and caressed each other with gentle strokes, the rest of the pub became a blur as both men became lost in each others eyes. Clive was about to say something, but was interrupted by the air raid siren. It must have been situated very close to the pub, because it drowned anything but the loudest shout. Roger leaned closer to Clive and shout-whispered into his ear, "Let's take a cab back to my flat." Clive nodded, and they stood up, grabbed their coats and bags, threw some cash on the table, and made for the door.

They held hands in the roomy darkness of the cab, and at one point Clive even rested his head on Roger's shoulder. When they got into Roger's neighborhood, he asked the cabby to let them off at the end of the street, and they walked the rest of the couple hundred yards. As they walked, they would occasionally hear the thud of bombs exploding far away, and could sometimes, but just barely, make out the droning hum of the Luftwaffe's planes high above London.

"Well, here we are," Roger whispered very close to Clive's ear. Although Clive had been here so much lately, it all felt totally new. Clive nodded as they turned to climb the stairs to the front door. Roger slipped a bent key into the door, pulled, and held it open for Clive. The door closed, and the sound of the city's sirens became muffled in the dry, dusty entrance hall.

"Remember to be careful of that top loose stair," Roger gently reminded, lighting one of the candles that sat on the table in the entranceway. The candlelight danced on Roger's handsome face, and Clive gently brushed a wave of hair from Roger's eyes. It was a delicate gesture, and one not missed by the shadows that danced and climbed the walls of the entrance hall. The two men quickly climbed the stairs to the door, and Roger almost dropped the keys in nervous excitement. By this time, each man had already removed his coat, dropping them on the floor as they entered the living room. As the door closed behind them they took each other, their mouths meeting in a blissful kiss. They seemed to fall into each other's arms, becoming one. Their bodies couldn't get any closer, and the candlelight shadowed the two as they melded into a phallic pillar standing alone on the worn Persian carpet near the door. Roger brought his hands up and caressed the back of Clive's head, feeling the dry silkiness of his short hair on the nape of his neck. His hands roamed slowly down Clive's back and around to his hips, and then gently up his strong arms. When he reached Clive's collar, he started to undo the buttons.

By this time Clive's hands were working, too, and he unbuttoned Roger's shirt and pushed it down so that it was hanging like a kilt from where it was tucked into his pants. Now both shirtless, they continued kissing, and Roger, whose smooth back was being stroked by Clive's strong but gentle hand, wished it would never end. Roger mentally cursed Clive's uniform for hiding his wonderful body—the wide shoulders that inverted to a narrow waist, the ever-so-slight washboard stomach, he strong pectorals and arms of someone who certainly exercised regularly. Roger felt Clive's mouth move to his ear.

"We'd probably be more comfortable in the bedroom?" he whispered in his beautiful English accent. Roger looked into Clive's face with a soft grin, and was surprised at how blue his eyes were up close. As Roger lifted the candle with one hand, the other slid into the top of Clive's pants and gently pulled him down the hallway. As they passed the bathroom, Clive grabbed the doorjamb, "I've just got to hit the head," Clive said quietly. "Don't start without me!"

"Don't worry," Roger whispered, handing him the burning candle. The two men smiled at each other, and Clive slowly raised his hand to the side of Roger's face, and instinctively, Roger tilted his head into it.

"Just don't take too long," Roger said as an afterthought. To the sound of Clive urinating, Roger walked in the darkness towards his bedroom. He realized that the sirens had stopped, and assumed that because so few bombs had been heard, the Luftwaffe's main targets must have been northward towards Coventry or Birmingham. By the time he saw the candlelight approaching from the hall, he was already undressed and in bed, lying on top of the comforter with his head propped up on pillows. Clive put the candle on the bench at the foot of the bed, slid out of the rest of his uniform, and sat next to Roger.

"Hello, you," Clive said, gently tracing Roger's face with his hand.

"Hello," Roger replied, pulling Clive on top of him.

Their lovemaking went on for hours, interrupted only by short periods of sleep and an occasional three-sentence conversation. Roger found a bliss he had known with no other man, and couldn't believe he had found Clive. In bed with his head on Clive's strong chest, listening to the slow, steady beat of a heart he yearned to keep, the faintest of morning light started to seep through the windows. Roger realized that unlike in his youth, he had actually grown more cynical, and had lost the idea that he could even think about settling down with one man, believing it instead to be an impossibility. Despite this, Roger started to seriously think about how it might be done with Clive. He also realized that what had happened the night before complicated not only their private lives, but just as importantly, their mission to retrieve Rotor IV. In his head, he suddenly heard his friend John's voice say, *you are certainly indestructible*. The voice quickly changed into his friend

Stephen's: *in leaps of faith, sometimes the hand that catches you will not be seen until after your feet have left the precipice.* Roger prayed that both were true.

He looked at his watch, it was almost six thirty. He quietly slid out of bed, and stood looking at Clive's beautiful face—the strong, square jaw, the tousled hair, and the almost perfectly sized ears. He would be lying to himself if he didn't admit to loving Clive, and he knew that he'd be lying, too, if he didn't also admit to having fallen in love with Clive that first afternoon in his office. Roger tiptoed to the kitchen and started breakfast.

Gotta keep my man fed, he thought. Startled by the musing, he looked up from the eggs and ham he was preparing on the stove, and smiled at the idea of someone being "his man." He went back to the task of preparing breakfast, only now he was whistling.

Chapter II: Schema

The old man, now finished with his cigarette, squeezed the lit head off and slid the butt into his pocket. Things had changed in the world, one of them being you couldn't drop trash on the ground, or flick your cigarette butts either; he liked the idea, and made it one of his principles. He stood up from the rock he had been sitting on, and felt the usual rush of searing pain in his left leg. He didn't mind, though, because it brought the old man back to him.

Their relationship quickly developed into a closeness both men had never known in previous affairs. They spent a great deal of their waking and sleeping moments together—their lovemaking was slow and sublime, their passion honest and gentle. Roger still found it hard to believe that he could be so smitten by Clive, but realized there could have been no other way—from the moment he had met Clive, he was in love. They worked ferociously on planning the retrieval of Rotor IV, putting in twelve-hours almost every day. This, however, did not exhaust their relationship, and by the time they made it back to Roger's flat each night, they were usually fully energized at the thought of once again being alone with each other.

Clive basically moved into Roger's apartment. It wasn't the result of a formal decision, but happened almost naturally, and when anyone asked, they said that Roger's flat was closer to the Admiralty, and that with the extra hours Clive was spending on the mission, it only made sense. Each night after they got home, having purchased their dinner from the pub down the block, Roger would throw the food on plates and rustle up some cutlery while Clive threw some wood in the fireplace and started a fire to warm the place up. The two would sit next to each other on the floor in front of the fire, eating and talking. Sometimes, one would tell a story and the other would laugh. Sometimes, one would tell a story and the other would reach out to place a reassuring hand on top of his. By now, having spent hours upon hours talking about their lives, Roger felt as if he had known Clive for years.

One night, as they were clearing away the plates after dinner, Roger thought to himself that where love fell so quickly and powerfully, it was necessary that there exist an immense relaying of personal information, so that the knowledge each had of the other could rise to the same level of intimacy they shared. Roger's parents had been married for twenty-four years, and yet his father had known very little about his mother, and on many occasions had forgotten such simple things as her middle name. That was not going to be the case here. Roger already knew so much about Clive's life that he felt he had watched it all at the cinema.

During one of their discussions, the conversation wended its way to Roger and Clive's past boyfriends. Clive had been telling Roger about his longer relationships, and had become somewhat sad and contemplative.

"And then there was Charlie, who I loved dearly," he said solemnly, "and who left me when… when… um, let's move on, shall we?" Clive had apparently hit a spot that he thought had healed enough to discuss, but was still too painful. Roger easily caught this, and quickly steered clear.

"So," Roger asked. "When you and William went your separate ways, you must have been quite angry?"

"Incensed," Clive said, revitalized. "Even though it was me who initiated our parting, the way he finished it was so enraging that I smashed a number of beautiful, though somewhat erotic, amphorae I had picked up in Greece. The place was littered with shards of naked men. Thank heavens for my man," Clive said laughing.

"Man?"

"Oh, my butler, who helped me clean it all up," Clive clarified. "Don't worry, he was sixty-three and ugly as sin. But, he didn't seem bothered by the occasional young man I'd bring in. I wonder what ever happened to Geoffrey?"

"Well, I know what you mean about being so peeved and all, but sometimes it comes with a mixture of both sorrow and pain, you know? Like, when Stephen broke up with me, I was very upset, though I didn't dare let him see it. I remember the day as if it was yesterday, mostly because it was the sunniest day you could imagine…"

The sun sparkled on the top of the water like a diamond necklace on black velvet, while the twenty-foot sailing boat silently cut through the waters of Boothbay Harbor. Roger was getting away from the factory after a month and a half of working almost non-stop at its helm., He had decided to take Stephen up on his offer to visit, despite the order from his father to stay away.

The night before, they had dined with Stephen's parents at their country club, then went to see a new movie, then back to the summerhouse where he and Stephen retired—sadly, to separate rooms. Roger was thrilled at being away from the factory and spending time with Stephen, made him so relaxed that he fell asleep almost instantly. That morning at breakfast, they decided to take the boat out for the day or, more to the point, Stephen decided they would take the boat out for the day. Roger, still overjoyed at being away from the factory, hadn't noticed that Stephen had barely touched him since his arrival the day before.

They had sailed all morning, and Roger finally began to notice an unusual reticence in Stephen. During their picnic lunch on the deck, Stephen barely said a word. By dessert, Roger couldn't take it anymore, and so confronted him.

"What's wrong, Stephen," Roger asked matter-of-factly. There was a very long pause, as Stephen stared out at the water.

"I'm sorry, Roger, I can't go on with this," Stephen finally said. He was facing away from Roger, looking toward the shore, his voice an amalgamation of anger and sadness. "The running around behind people's back, the effort

involved in being so secretive—I can't take it any longer. I'm seriously thinking of asking Madeline Klein, who as you know I've also been seeing, to marry me."

"Stephen, you can't be serious." Roger was more surprised than hurt. "What are you saying?"

"I'm saying I can't be your, well, friend, anymore. If we continued to see each other even under what would be considered normal circumstances, the pain for both of us would be unbearable."

"Stephen, what's going on?" Roger demanded. "This is certainly not like you."

"As I said, I'm tired of living this charade, and I don't have the energy to do this for the rest of my life. Let's just leave it at that, okay?"

It was just like Stephen to trap him on the boat to tell him it was over.

"It's getting cold out here. Let's go back in," Stephen said after several minutes of silence. Roger remained quiet, staring out into the harbor at the small sails that dotted the horizon. His heart was breaking, but he was Roger Mathews and would let no man see him cry. They would go back to the house, he would put on a wonderful performance in front of Stephen's parents, saying something to the extent that he was urgently needed back at the factory. Even now, though, his stoic demeanor betrayed his total grief and fear. He knew there was something that Stephen wasn't telling him, and this only heightened the pain he felt. They got back to shore, wordlessly tied the boat, and walked back to the house. Unable to walk together, Roger walked up the yard from the boathouse first, followed ten yards behind by Stephen. They found Stephen's parents on a veranda sipping vodka martinis, and Roger explained that he was being called back on urgent business. It didn't take Roger long to pack and throw his valise into the back of his open car. He turned and looked at Stephen, who was doing a superb job of acting as if nothing was wrong—he was almost smiling. Roger's eyes didn't leave Stephen as he slid into the driver's seat. He slowly turned to face the long driveway, and leaned forward to start the car. Looking up and into the distance, he slowly shook his head, shifted into gear, and drove away.

It would be many years before Roger would find out that as his car disappeared behind the last tall border of topiary, Stephen, standing so small on the graveled driveway, had broken into tears. That from his back trouser pocket, he had pulled the intimidating and threatening letter from Roger's father, which clearly spelled out Stephen's personal downfall and his family's shame should he continue seeing Roger. That, through a kaleidoscope of tears, he had looked up from the letter and whispered "I'm sorry, Roger," toward the diminishing sound of Roger's car...

"Roger? Roger?" It was Clive, standing in his kitchen, scraping some food from a plate into the rubbish bin. "It looked like you left us for a while," he joked. "You were telling me about, what was his name, Stephen, I believe?"

"Uh, yes, well, he ended things rather abruptly," Roger said, swirling the remaining wine in his glass and gulping it down.

"It doesn't matter, we are here now, just you and me," Clive said, walking over and putting his arms around Roger's waist, clasping his hands at the small of Roger's back, their faces inches apart. "And I think you make up for all the hell I've gone through before."

"I'll second that," Roger whispered, leaning in and kissing Clive. It was slow, and passionate, and filled with deep affection. Roger looked into Clive's crystal eyes.

"Clive, you don't think we're moving too fast on this, do you?" he asked, trying hard not to sound too vulnerable, but more importantly, not wanting to alarm Clive. "It's just that we've known each other for only three weeks. I know we both feel as if it's been much longer. It's certainly not that I want this to end, but that's why I'm worried. I don't want it to end. I don't want it to ever end."

Clive looked into Roger's sea-blue eyes, reached up and slid the back of his hand gently down the side of Roger's face to his chin, where his hand stopped, then he leaned in and tenderly kissed Roger.

"No, Roger," Clive gently said, sounding wonderfully seductive with his upper-class British accent. "We are not moving too fast, we're simply making up for lost time."

Roger thought about that for a moment, decided that he liked the answer, and leaned in for another long kiss. Their lovemaking that night was short, yet maintained the fiery passion that had become a standard for them.

"Oh, I forgot to tell you," Clive said after they finished and were lying in bed. "I just found out that my parents are in the Bletchley Park area visiting my mother's cousin, and as we've already planned to motor there tomorrow to see Alan, I was thinking of visiting them. However, that leaves you in a position of getting home on your own—that is, unless you want to come with me?"

"Thanks, but no thanks," Roger replied smiling. "I'd prefer not to have to meet your father, and there's a train that I can take back to London, anyway."

"Fine then, after we meet with Alan, I'll continue on to see my parents. I'll probably spend the night and return to London the following day." Clive thought for a moment, and then added, "It's so bittersweet, you know, wanting to see my mother, yet also not wanting to see my father."

"I know, Clive, I'm sorry about that, but you'll see me when you get back, and I'll make it up to you." He turned over and laid his head on Clive's broad, bare chest.

They were both sound asleep in minutes.

The next morning was dank and rainy when Clive picked up the car he had secured through the Royal Navy. Then he came back to pick up Roger, and the two were off for Bletchley Park. Roger wanted to drive, and Clive gave no argument, wanting instead to take a nap. After they got themselves out of London, Clive quickly leaned his head to the side and was asleep in minutes. Roger drove on, thinking about what he was going to say to Clive concerning his tryst with Alan the year before.

Over the past couple of weeks they had both discussed their earlier relationships, but those conversations ended or steered a different course before Roger had ever gotten the chance to mention Alan. Not that Roger thought Clive would be bothered by it, but it was something he knew Clive should know about. Still, it wasn't an easy thing to bring up, because the previously discussed boyfriends were all in the past, and Alan was here in the present, and the three would be working together..

Roger drove on, maneuvering the car around potholes and bumps in the weathered road that meandered through the dreary English countryside. When they were near enough to Bletchley Park, Roger tactfully drove the car over, rather than around, a large, rain-filled pot hole in the road, which did its job in jostling Clive awake.

"Well good morning, sleepy head."

"Ugggh," Clive said, trying to wake up. "How far away are we?"

"We should be there soon." Roger waited a few minutes before talking further, to allow Clive a bit of time to wake up.

"Clive, there's something I need to tell you."

"Not much good can come from something starting with that line," shifting in his seat to look at Roger.

"No, don't worry, it's not something drastic. I just wanted to tell you something about Alan and me."

"Go on, then."

"Well, when I first arrived and started working at the embassy, and going to Bletchley Park and spending time with Alan, we kind of had a very short…tryst, I guess is how you can put it. It ended really quickly, but unlike earlier relationships I've had, it left us really good friends. I just thought you should know."

"Well, to be honest with you, I had heard a rumor about Professor Turing, and it just surprises me that you'd take the chance with someone whose proclivities are not as secret as the rest of us."

"Well, at my urging," Roger defended himself, "it was carefully kept very quiet. Again, it ended very quickly, only a couple of weeks."

"Don't get me wrong, Roger, I can see how it could happen. Alan is attractive, and he's a nice fellow. What's not to like?"

"Are you bothered that we're still good friends?"

"No, not at all. I trust you, Roger." Clive said, looking at Roger, his face tensing, then relaxing with a smile.

"Thanks, Clive," Roger said, sliding his hand off the gear stick and into Clive's.

They finally arrived at Bletchley Park. Roger showed his pass to the guard at the gate, and followed the narrow driveway to Hut Number 8, a single story longhouse whose simplicity of design left little doubt that it had been hastily built. There were many of the structures scattered around the main mansion, all filled with people trying to either solve the Enigma riddle or to use known decoding methods to make at least partial sense of recently acquired Nazi messages. Clive followed Roger as they made their way to Alan's office door. Roger knocked twice and opened it without waiting for a response.

"Roger, how are you?" Alan exclaimed, coming around from behind his desk and shaking Roger's hand. "I never see you anymore. I shall sue you for abandonment." Roger knew that if Clive hadn't been with him, he would have been greeted with a bear hug.

"That's not true, Alan," Roger corrected. "We saw each other at the meeting at the Admiralty just three weeks ago."

"Yes, but that's still too long. Besides, I meant visiting me here, not merely seeing each other in some stuffy meeting chamber."

"Well, there you have me," Roger conceded. "You remember

Captain Westmore?" Roger put his hand on Clive's back and urged him forward.

"Ah, yes, Captain, how are you?" He reached out and shook Clive's hand.

"Please, call me Clive."

"And you call me Alan. So, Clive, I take it you'll soon be behind enemy lines? How positively exciting. I'm almost envious." Alan smiled, impishly rubbing his hands together.

"Don't be," Roger interjected with a hint of annoyance at his old friend. "It's very dangerous."

"Oh, I'm sure, I'm sure," Alan said soothingly. "Honestly, though, it is an honor working with you, Clive."

"Likewise," Clive said. "I've actually heard a lot about you and your work."

The three sat down and Alan spent a great deal of time going over how Clive would be able to tell if the Enigma rotor he was given was a dummy. It was an informative lesson, and one that would prove important if Clive got to the rendezvous point and realized the French had stumbled onto a faux rotor. Afterward, Roger and Clive gave Alan a brief rundown of how the mission was expected to unfold.

"I have one tremendously large favor to ask of you, though," Alan said when they were finished. "It is a big favor, but I need your help."

"Certainly, Alan," Roger responded. "What is it?"

"Well, I have recently come up with a small device that allows me to attach a radio transmitter or receiver to my copy of the Enigma machine. It's a very primitive piece that in the future could help decode messages as the radio signal is being intercepted. You see, the way it's down now is that radio signals with encrypted messages are intercepted, put on paper, and then sent to the decipherer, who decodes the message, and sends it back to wherever—it's very laborious and bureaucratic. However, if the message could be received and decoded on the spot, a lot of time would be saved. Again, my device is rather primitive and prototypical, but I need to get close enough to German transmission points to test it."

"That would make sense," Roger said, nodding and looking at Alan.

"Well, the problem is that this device is very important to me, but I can't actually perform tests on it because I'm here, nowhere near Nazi radio points of transmission. So, I was hoping, praying, actually, that you would let me come on the ship that transports Clive to France, and test it on the radio transmissions emitting from the coast of France." When he finished, he looked sheepishly from Roger to Clive, then back to Roger.

"Oh, I don't know," Clive said, sounding dubious. "I'd be open for it, but we'll have to put a formal request into the Admiralty for such a thing."

"Well, you see, therein lies the problem," Alan countered. "I was hoping that because this device I've come up with is so new—even my superiors aren't aware of it—that I could have the chance to test it out before I formally present it to them."

A moment of silence passed, with Alan again looking back and forth between Roger and Clive.

"Well," Roger said, turning to Clive, "I think it can be allowed. After all, it's just for the ride out and back, and it doesn't sound like he would be in anyone's way."

"I know," Clive answered. "However, I'm more concerned about what would happen if something went wrong."

Alan sat silently, letting Clive and Roger volley back and forth, knowing that Roger would come through for him.

"Well, let's see," Roger began. "The worst that could happen is that the ship would be captured and boarded, in which case Alan could just throw his Enigma machine overboard. Furthermore, Alan is British, so it wouldn't complicate one of our main objectives, which is to make sure the Nazis are unaware of American involvement."

"I'm still not sure," Clive said, rubbing his chin.

"Look, Clive, the chance of anything happening to the ship is very low. You've said this yourself."

"But I don't like not having such a thing listed, or put on paper, that's all."

"My test is all receiving transmissions…" Alan now thought it best to interject. "And there's no way the Nazis could detect a thing."

"Come on, Clive," Roger said. "I'll accept full responsibility on this one."

"Well, then, I guess it can be allowed," Clive said. "I will, however, make him an honorary crew member, which at least makes *me* feel a little better."

"Oh, thank you," Alan proclaimed. "Thank you so much. This will really help me test this device, which I'm very excited about, but haven't dared tell anyone in fear that it wouldn't live up to expectations."

"I'll arrange for you to get to Pevensey, the small coastal town from where the boat will launch," Roger told Alan. "I may even come and pick you up myself."

"Oh, this is all so splendid," Alan said, smiling at Clive and Roger. "I can't thank you enough. Won't you both please join me for lunch?"

Clive graciously declined. "I'm afraid I have to see my parents. They're visiting friends in the area."

"Oh, and you're going, too?" Alan asked, turning to Roger.

"No," Roger said. "I'm going back to London by train later this afternoon."

"Well, then, that leaves you and me, Roger," Alan proposed with an impish smile. Roger turned to look at Clive, who smiled and winked, letting him know it was perfectly fine with him.

"I would be delighted," Roger said, turning and smiling back at Alan. "Where did you have in mind?"

"Well, we could risk Bletchley Park's commissary," Alan said, "but there's a small out-of-the-way place that's, well, not too far out-of-the-way. Shall we give it a go, then?"

After seeing Clive to his car, and a brief good-bye, Roger and Alan set off for the pub. The place was small, dark, and charming, and the ale they ordered came quickly. As they waited for their first course, during a lull in what had been up to that point an ordinary conversation about how dreadful the weather had been lately, Alan leaned in closer, looked straight into Roger's face and asked, "So, how long have you and Clive been sleeping together?"

"What makes you think we're sleeping together?" Roger asked, looking around to make sure no one heard.

"Oh, please, Roger, it's about as apparent as a stiff percy," Alan shot back. "Just look at the two of you! Neither of you can pass by the other without putting your hands on them and gently moving them out of the way; whatever happened to a simple 'excuse me?' Secondly, your concern about Clive in France is obvious and at a level that is much too high for the Roger Mathews that I know. Lastly, you have this glow about you, Roger, that I've never seen before—it's bloody disgusting, I'll tell you. I'm envious, though, he's a real looker. You should keep him."

"I intend to," Roger smiled, admitting to the relationship.

"Oh, my God! Does he know about you and me?"

"The truth is easier than keeping secrets," Roger answered, leaning closer across the table. "I think I'm in love, Alan, but it's scary. I've never felt this way before."

"Roger, I'm hurt," Alan jokingly pouted. "Not even with me?"

"Please, Alan, I'm serious," Roger said earnestly. "And we're planning on sending him into Nazi-occupied France, and I'm torn to pieces because of it. Alan, if anything happens to him I don't know what I'd do."

"Well, then, you must simply plan for every contingency," Alan said, now seriously. "Don't worry, Roger, he'll return to you. Of this, I'm certain." Then Alan showed his impish smile and asked, "So, tell me, is he good in bed?"

Roger couldn't help smiling at his friend's tawdry audacity.

After lunch with Alan, Roger made his way to the train station and caught the late afternoon train back to London. He was alone in his seat, sitting across from a young boy of about ten years old, reading a book, and sitting next to a frumpish woman who looked very stern and solemn. A lot of children could be seen on trains lately, but usually arriving there in Buckinghamshire, where Bletchley was located, or heading further north, as many families decided their children would be safer outside of London. They would be taken in by families enlisted to care for these evacuated children until the bombs stopped falling... *though God only knew when that would be*, Roger thought, as he and the boy looked at each other.

"Are you going to London?" the boy asked.

"Yes, actually I am," Roger gently replied.

"I'm going back to London, too," said the boy quietly. "My Mum and Dad were killed by a bomb two days ago, and the funeral is tomorrow." Roger's horrified eyes met those of the older woman, and she nodded.

"'Tis a nasty business, this bombing," she said. "This is Robert, and the son of my dead sister and her husband, God rest their souls—God rest all their souls."

"Oh, Robert, I'm so sorry," Roger said to the boy, so thrown off that he forgot he was speaking to a child and sounded more as if he was giving condolences to an adult. Catching himself, he added, "A lot of people are dying in this war, Robert, but there are many people working hard to make sure what happened to your mother and father doesn't happen to other children's parents. I'm sorry that it wasn't in time to save yours."

The three became quiet, and the boy went back to his book, and the old lady closed her eyes and rested. Roger turned again to stare out the window of the train. *This war has to be won*, he thought to himself. It's one thing to lose a father in battle, which is bad enough, but this was the twentieth century. Had the world come so far and made so much progress in every facet of society, culture, and modernity, and yet still allow a war that caused the deaths of so many innocent civilians? The tear-like droplets of rain streaked across the window as the train chugged along. He felt very small, and wished Clive had not gone to his parents, but was with him now.

He couldn't sleep that night, thinking about the boy he'd talked to on the train, and so allowed himself yet again to be lured to the rooftop to watch an air raid. Bundled warmly in his thick coat, his mind dwelt on death, and war, and Clive. Despite the boy's parents dying in a bombing, Roger thought about the many who remained in London and spent their nights in the subway stations of the Underground. The bombing raids continued, and Londoners went about their day as usual, almost as if the air raids were simply a new form of inclement weather. Roger appreciated this characteristic of the English—genteel and civilized as a rule, but strong, bold, and courageous in the face of danger or threat.

It was one of the reasons he loved Clive. Despite his aristocratic background, Clive was physically quite strong and, to a certain extent, rugged. His arms and stomach were quite powerful, yet he was so gentle, so sweet. His usually hearty voice could become so soft and halcyon that its juxtaposition with his solid body was explosively attractive. It had been almost four weeks now since they'd met, and yet it felt as if they had been friends forever. Roger hadn't given much thought in several years to settling down, hadn't paid much attention to the idea that there could be such a thing as the "right man," but he was slowly beginning to reconsider. He was getting edgy though, knowing that they were putting the final touches on their mission, which would put Clive in occupied France within the next few days. He dreaded the idea, and wanted to escape thinking about it, but because his work centered on the mission, it was difficult to get his mind away from it.

"Elizabeth," Roger called to his secretary, turning from his desk and speaking down the passage to where she sat. "Could you bring me file K3-2118, please?"

He turned back to the work on his desk. Clive wasn't getting back into town until later that day, so he took the opportunity to get a lot of his own preparations done. Occasionally he would close the door and make a phone call to Admiral Welles, or to one of the few others who knew of their mission. Elizabeth, as well as Clive's secretary, knew nothing of their plan, but must have known something was up because of the amount of overtime they were recently required to work.

"Here's the file," Elizabeth said entering his sun-filled office.

"Fine, thanks," turning back to his work. Although the plan was basically set, they were now simply putting all the pieces together before the mission. The plan was rather straightforward, and it fit on a single page of paper clipped to the inside of his main folder:

1. Wednesday: 2300 hours—The landing ship carrying Captain Westmore and three small trucks filled with the ammunition and supplies lands on the French coast just south of Boulogne-Sur-Mer. Captain Westmore to meet up with his guide from the French Resistance, who will have with him two drivers to drive the two other trucks.

2. Thursday: 0100 hours—Captain Westmore and the French Resistance team arrive in the small city of Abbeville, where

they are to deliver the first truck to other members of the French Resistance.

3. Thursday: 0330 hours—Delivery of the next truckload of supplies to the second town, Amiens. This second town is dangerous, and will require more carefulness because it houses the region's Nazi Command post, and so is teaming with the enemy.

4. Thursday: 0500 hours—They will have delivered all three trucks to all three towns, the last of which is Arras, the furthest most point they would penetrate into enemy territory. Captain Westmore and the guide will wait the day out in Arras. Sometime during that day, they will be delivered the Enigma rotor.

5. Thursday: 2200 hours—Captain Westmore and his guide begin their trek back to the rendezvous point on the coast.

6. Friday 0300 hours—Captain Westmore will be picked up and returned safely with the rotor.

Of course, this was the basic plan, and each of the six points contained several factors, some very complex and requiring careful precision in both timing and execution, and there was constant room for fine tuning, correction, and overrule. Slowly, though, his mind wandered to a different place away from plans of war…

Roger lay on the cool cotton sheets, listening to John's rhythmic breathing. They had enjoyed a wonderful night together. They had driven into Cambridge to have dinner with some of John's friends, then to Boston to walk around and enjoy the warm summer night. They talked a lot that evening — about plans for the future, their future — and it sounded nice. They would move into the same apartment building, preferably in apartments that were next to each other, and there they would live basically together. Roger's father was already suspicious of their friendship, and Roger realized that he couldn't make a single friend without his father assuming that it was a love affair. They sipped coffee at a quaint eatery they found in Old Town, and then held hands in the car on their ride back. They returned to John's apartment and kissed each other in John's bedroom, where they made love, and fell asleep in each other's arms.

And now Roger lay awake thinking about the plans he and John had made the night before, and how implausible they were while his father was still alive. The idea of letting his father disown him did enter his mind — that it might be better than living in fear — but he had grown accustomed to living in a privileged world, where coming out would be his complete end. And so he chose to live on the periphery, love the men he loved, and occasionally take out the pretty little beard whenever things seemed too hot, or if he got wind of social gossip about his perpetual bachelorhood.

The best laid plans of mice and men, he thought, as he rolled away from John and out of bed.

Roger met Clive at noon that day in front of the Admiralty building. It was the first time the two had been apart for more than twenty-four hours, and it was like the reunion of two little boys whose summers were spent apart because one had been at summer camp.

"Hey," Roger said, giving Clive a fake jab to the shoulder. "Hope you had a good trip."

"Hello," Clive said back, going for a fake block. "I did, thanks."

"How are your parents?" Roger asked, looking somewhat serious now. "Did your father behave himself?"

"Mother's fine, but as to my father, no. We had, oh, about five separate rows, each progressively worse." The two men started walking to the cab Roger had ordered to stay and wait for him. "I was saved because we were not at Blythdale, and so he had to be on his best behavior, which as you can guess isn't very good."

"Well, at least you're back with me, now." They climbed into the back of the cab.

"The Dorchester Hotel, please, cabby," Roger said, leaning forward towards the driver. He slid the privacy partition closed, then sat back and spoke quietly to Clive. "We're still on with Jean Pierre in half an hour to firm plans for when you land, and we have a meeting with Admiral Welles at four o'clock…oh, and I just received notice this morning that Pomboi from the FBI will be there, too."

"Pomboi? Oh, that's right, he was at the first meeting, right?"

"Yes, so you remember him. I hear he's actually forty-six, but he really looks a lot older. I was first introduced to him by the Embassy's Chief of Staff just before that first meeting at the Admiralty, so he must hold some level of influence. Either way, I didn't much care for him. He's full of himself, much too cocky, and I wouldn't be surprised to find out that when he was a boy, he pulled the wings off of insects."

"I though he seemed somewhat dour, myself," Clive said, then changed the subject. "As to Jean Pierre, has he determined who my guide will be? That is crucial, and I'm somewhat concerned that he hasn't the slightest idea who he'll have as a guide."

"Well, Clive," Roger explained jokingly, "that's the French for you, they'll keep you hanging to the last minute."

"Yes, however, it's that word 'hanging' that leaves me feeling somewhat uncomfortable," Clive said, joking back.

In twenty minutes they were in room 623 of the Dorchester waiting for Jean Pierre to arrive. Not long after, there was a knock at the door, and Clive opened it for the handsome Frenchman.

"Gentlemen, good afternoon," Jean Pierre said in French.

"It is good to see you, Jean Pierre. Can I offer you some tea, or perhaps coffee," Clive replied in flawlessly native French.

"Thank you," Jean Pierre said. "Tea, please." They sat at the small table near the window. "Have you collected the needed inventory, messieurs? I have made sure that the rotor is safe and in good keeping in my hometown of Arras, and your guide, Monsieur Captain, is one of our best. I am certain you will be in the best of hands."

"Good," Roger said, and realized that maybe he wasn't the one who should have responded, and that it was probably said with a little too much concern. The Frenchman picked up on this, and smiled. "Again, Monsieur Roger, your friend will be safe with our guide, who is one of the bravest we have."

"We have collected all the supplies you asked for," Clive said, sliding a paper across to Jean Pierre. "The three lorries will be disguised as bread trucks, and will have all the necessary documents and forged clearances as currently demanded by the Vichy government in France. Inside, secret compartments will hold all of the materials you request, and these will be hidden by fake walls of fresh bread. After reaching each town, the trucks will simply be surrendered to your people, and the convoy will continue to the next town."

The meeting continued for half an hour, and finished at two-thirty. When it was done, all was in place for the actual mission to flow as planned. After Jean Pierre left, the two moved to the sitting area of the hotel room, and sat on one of the two opposing love seats.

"What time did you say our meeting was with the admiral?" Clive asked, looking up at the clock above the gilded fireplace.

"Four o'clock. Why?" Roger followed Clive's gaze to above the mantle.

"And how long does it take to get to the Admiralty from here?" Clive further queried, but with a rather jocular tone in his voice.

"Well, I'd guess it's only about five minutes from…" Roger stopped in mid-sentence. "Oh, I see where you're headed with this. Was your next question going to be something about how we might spend the next hour before we have to leave for the

Admiralty?"

"Yes, it was," Clive smiled back, sliding his hand over the sofa's velvety cushion and into Roger's hand.

"And maybe you were going to add that it's such a shame this hotel room has been paid for, and all it was used for was a forty-five minute meeting?" Roger said, as he slid next to Clive.

"Yes, that, too," Clive whispered, their faces leaning into each other, just inches apart.

"Well then, Captain," Roger softly said, "maybe we should do something about that."

Roger's lips met Clive's, and he began undoing the buttons of Clive's creaseless, white uniform. He pulled the shirt back to expose Clive's strong, hairless stomach and chest. They stood up to slowly and intimately remove each other's clothing. Soon, the two were completely naked, standing and kissing in front of the room's fireplace. Roger saw their beauty in the reflection of the mirror above the mantle.

"Clive?" Roger asked, putting his head on Clive's smooth shoulder.

"Yes, my love. What is it?"

"I don't want you to go to France."

"Well, if you're afraid I won't come back to you, you're wrong," Clive said calmly. "Look, Roger." He drew back to hold Roger's face in his hands. "I've been on many missions, some riskier than this. I promise, I will bring myself back, and you and I will have a lovely little private dinner to celebrate."

Roger looked for a moment into Clive's eyes, then slowly nodded his head. Clive leaned in and kissed Roger, who kissed back. Their lovemaking was beautiful, but Roger's mind was still on Clive being sent into occupied France, on a mission that could end with him captured, or even executed if the Nazis deemed it necessary.

They were dressed and at the Admiralty building right on time. The affable Admiral Welles and stern FBI Agent Pomboi seemed an interesting juxtaposition of personalities Roger thought, as he and Clive were shown into Welles' large office by his secretary. Pomboi was sitting in a large, over-stuffed chair, his moderate frame slouched comfortably back as he stirred the contents of a small teacup. His posture and movement seemed fluid and genteel, but his face, which was grimly weathered, was like a stone-cold beacon casting a cold light on those who looked into it.

Pomboi did not get up when the two young men entered. The admiral sat behind his massive desk, which Roger had noticed during earlier meetings rather looked like a ship unto itself. It had intricate carvings and designs, and the soft, flattened felt beneath the glass top shimmered sea green, giving it even more of an oceanic feeling. It was a mysterious piece, which seemed to hide a secret somewhere in its carved vines and fantastic animals. The admiral nodded in response to Clive's salute, and waved the men into chairs across from the desk.

"Then we are set, gentlemen," Welles said, leaning back in his chair. "Agent Pomboi and I have reviewed your plans, and everything seems to be in shape for the mission's execution. Though, we do have a few questions... Agent Pomboi?"

"I was just wondering," Pomboi said, almost snidely, "what your plans were in the event that you were captured by the Germans. Although you give one or two scenarios in your mission plan, out of curiosity, can you go into, well, greater detail?"

"Certainly," Clive started. "If we are captured, sir, I would most likely be taken as a French Resistance fighter. My mother was French, and I was raised speaking both English and French, so I speak perfect French. Now, depending on what point in the mission a capture would take place, would prescribe what would probably happen, and how I would handle the matter. Also, a lot would depend on the number of German soldiers who were present. Shall I continue?"

"Please do," Pomboi said emotionlessly.

"For instance, if we are caught with all three trucks, but there were only two Nazi soldiers, we would attempt to eradicate them and move on with our mission. British Intelligence has already shown that it is rare, but not uncommon, for Nazi soldiers to disappear for a day or two, usually with a local French girl. When they report back to base, they have their wrists slapped, and that's that. So, the liquidation of up to four Nazi soldiers could go unnoticed for enough time for us to be well out of the area."

"And if it were a large regiment of, say, twelve Nazis?" Pomboi posed.

"Then I blend in with the others as resistance fighters, and hope the most they'd do is interrogate me and throw me in a prison camp," Clive said, matter-of-factly.

"Yes, well, wouldn't that be lovely?" Pomboi said, sarcastically. "I'm more concerned about the inevitable interrogation. What do you say there?" As Pomboi seemed to be directing all of his questions to Clive, Roger remained silent, nodding his head in agreement to the answers Clive was giving. He was once again put off by the FBI agent's cold and menacing personality, and his mistrust of Pomboi was continuing to grow.

"We tell them basically the truth," answered Clive, "so far as the ammunition and goods are concerned, that we received them as a gift from the English."

Now it was the admiral who spoke. "Where would you tell them you were going, and where would you tell them you had been given the supplies?"

"We would tell them the truth about the first two towns we intend to go to, but not wanting to risk the rotor, we would give them an erroneous town for the third," Clive explained.

"And why wouldn't the other French members of your team cough up the truth?" Pomboi asked.

"Because, sir, the only one who would know the whole plan is the guide," Clive answered. "The others will be ignorant, mostly for their own safety, and they will follow orders as we give them. They wouldn't know about the final goal, which is getting the rotor."

The questioning went on for three quarters of an hour, with both Clive and Roger able to hold their own nicely through the onslaught of questions. Having planned very carefully, they proved their itinerary and stratagem to the satisfaction of both Admiral Welles and Agent Pomboi, who pressed his thin lips together and leaned back in his chair. After a few brief words of thanks, the admiral stood and shook Roger and Clive's hands, while Pomboi, still sitting, simply tilted his head in acknowledgement of their good-byes.

"Well, that went rather well," Clive said as they left the building onto the cold streets of Whitehall.

"True," Roger replied over his shoulder, hand raised trying to hail a cab. "But that Pomboi is sure a winner. Jeez, where'd they dig this guy up, a Frankenstein movie?" Roger half-joked.

"Well, he is rather stern and, somewhat eerie, I must say," Clive agreed, laughing.

"I don't know. There's something about him I don't trust. I can't place my finger on it. And is it me, or are you picking up an accent from him?"

"All you Yanks have accents," Clive said chuckling. A rotund checkered cab pulled up in front of them, and they jumped in.

"Grosvenor Square, please," Roger said, leaning toward the cabby, and then back towards Clive. "I don't know. I'm picking up an accent — ever so slight. I think it's French. You have to admit, Pomboi sounds French, right? Right? Clive?" Roger turned to see Clive leaning back against his rolled up trench coat, his eyes closed, his round lips smiling in pretend sleep.

"Okay," Roger jokingly scolded, "be that way."

Roger, now smiling himself, turned to look out the window as they passed street corners filled with sandbagged barricades and storefront windows taped and shuttered. Some streets had sidewalks that were impassable because of rubble from bombed out buildings. Roger turned again to look at his friend, how content he looked, how calm, even though he was being sent to a strange place in four days. He loved Clive so much that it scared him. But he'd just as soon lose an arm than lose that butterfly-in-the-stomach feeling he got whenever he saw Clive. As the cab continued through grimy streets to Roger's flat, he wished he had met Clive under different circumstances, but rejoiced in meeting him at all.

CHAPTER III: DILEMMA

The old man started walking upward from the spot he had been occupying. He had been hesitant, because the move would take him to their favorite spot, where they would often stand and watch the ocean, and talk, and reminisce about their life together. It was hard to believe they lasted so long, but they had made that plan long ago, during the war. The old man liked plans, and had stuck to most of them through hell and high water.

The morning sun streamed through the small window that sat high on the wall above the bathtub. It glistened in the water and lit the porcelain at the bottom of the tub, not unlike the way the sun dances at the bottom of a swimming pool, and this was why Roger liked to take his bath in the morning around this time. He would try to get the water very hot by pouring in a large vat of water he would heat on the stove. He was reading the London Times, and trying hard not to get the paper wet. Clive walked into the bathroom wearing a pair of dark plaid pajama pants and no shirt, showing off his thin waist and strong torso. "What's the news today?" he asked, brushing his teeth.

"Rising levels of lost tonnage from all parts of the United Kingdom at the hands of the German navy," Roger said solemnly. "It's not looking good, Clive. We have to get that rotor."

"We'll see if we can take care of that in three days," Clive said, turning to look at Roger. "And in five days I'll be back, we'll have the rotor, and you and I will have to find some nice reason to explain the amount of time we'll still be spending together." Clive dropped his pajama pants to the floor, exposing a rear that would put Di Vinci's David to shame. He walked over and sat on the lip of the bathtub.

"I'm scared for you, Clive. You'll know where you are at every step of the way, but I won't, you'll know that you're safe, but I won't. You see?"

"Roger, darling, I promise you as I have many times now, I will come back," Clive said soothingly. "Right now, our duty is to the mission. My return is secondary to its successful completion, and if you think about it, a successful completion ensures my return."

Clive stood and gently eased into the hot water, settling down and facing Roger from the other end of the large bathtub, the water level rising almost to the top of the tub. Roger liked it when Clive joined him — there was certainly enough room, and he loved the way Clive's wet skin glistened in the sun, accentuating every muscle underneath. Roger's mind went from nervousness to arousal as he watched Clive grab a sponge and start massaging his arm and shoulder.

"Need help?" Roger asked with a slight grin.

Clive smiled back, handed Roger the sponge, and turned around in the tub so that he could slide back, almost sitting in Roger's lap.

"I'm going to miss you," Roger said softly, as he waved the sponge over Clive's broad shoulders. "Who am I going to yell at to get the hell out of bed?"

"Well, it's only for two nights. Hey, Roger, maybe we should take a holiday in a week or two after I get back from the mission, head up to the Lake District. Or maybe we can go to my family's estate at Blythdale, visit my parents and give you a taste of what I've been telling you about them."

"That sounds good." Roger leaned forward and rested his cheek on Clive's moist back.

"You'll love my bachelor's suite at Blythdale. Two bedrooms, a large bathroom, small kitchen. It's a wonder I ever leave it when I'm there."

"Let's just get you back safe and sound," Roger murmured, pulling Clive towards him so that he slid further down in the tub, his back and head resting on Roger's chest. Clive slowly stroked

Roger's wet arm.

"When this mission is over," Roger said softly, "then we'll worry about going somewhere together."

The next day, Clive left early for Pevensey, the small coastal village from which they would launch their mission. He was to meet and review the plans with the captain of the landing vessel that would ferry him and the three trucks of ammunition and supplies across the English Channel. Roger stayed in London to meet with Admiral Welles, and pick up all the falsified documents and papers Clive would need. He would then drive to Bletchley Park to meet up with Alan, load up the car with the Enigma machine Alan wanted to test, and the two would drive to Pevensey to meet up with Clive.

Roger looked out of the cab's window at the melancholy streets of London. It was almost March, the weather cold and wet, and Roger's mood reflected that weather. Groups of black umbrellas rolled by like ominous clouds, and the burned-out neighborhoods the cab drove through reminded Roger that this was not a happy time, but instead one filled with peril and fear. He wanted the mission to be finished, he wanted Clive back safe and sound, and he wanted this dreaded war to be over.

The cab left him off in front of the large Admiralty building, its thick stone and brick façade stained wet under the windows by the rainy mist, giving the impression that it had been weeping. He walked in the golden glow of the hallways, passing doors that emitted the constant tap-tapping of typewriters. His briefcase felt heavy, and Roger wasn't sure if it was because of the extra papers that had accumulated over the past few weeks, or maybe his lack of sleep, or that he was nervous about the mission. He walked to the admiral's office, and was told that he had been called away for a while, that he would be back in fifteen minutes, and that Roger should go in and wait for him.

Roger entered the admiral's office, resting his briefcase on the floor near one of the two chairs that sat in front of the intricately carved ship-desk that he had been admiring for weeks now. He walked up to the desk and strolled around it, his hand gently tracing the carved bevel that ran its perimeter. The wood was old, he thought, and worm-eaten, but was nonetheless an amazing piece of furniture. The green felt underneath the glass top had faded in spots, which gave the desktop the impression of different depths. As he continued to admire the desk, despite the many files that sat on top of it, his eye immediately darted to "Roger Mathews" on a piece of paper that sat on top of an opened folder. He was amazed at the brain's ability to pick out one's own written name from a cacophony of words, sentences, and paragraphs that might otherwise conceal it. The folder it was sitting on was resting on top of a pile of similar folders, none of which seemed to have any logical order.

Neatly affixed at the top right-hand corner of the paper was a large red "Top Secret." Roger, leaving the document and its folder still on the desk, began reading:

From: Agent Milton Pomboi, U.S. Federal Agent, FBI

To: Admiral James Welles, HMS Navy

Enigma Mission: Update

Date February 28, 1941

Alpha and Beta teams are set with Captain James Pendington of His Majesty's Navy, and Mr. Charles Van Garten of the FBI. Captain Pendington is set to rendezvous with the French Resistance members with the actual Enigma Rotor IV in the town of Corbie on March 1, 1941 at 21:00 hrs.

The decoy Beta Team, consisting of Captain Clive Westmore of His Majesty's Navy, and Mr. Roger Mathews of the United States Embassy have planned for Captain Westmore to rendezvous with the French Resistance members with the decoy Enigma rotor in Arras. Neither man is suspicious of their false mission, and deceptive messages have been sent by several means so as to divert the Germans to the decoy agent. All incoming reconnaissance suggests that these misleading messages have been successful in throwing off the Nazis, and that they are only aware of Beta Team's plan, and therefore Alpha Team should well succeed in returning the actual Rotor IV.

At our request, the French Resistance leaders have deliberately misinformed their contact dealing with the Beta Team, and he, too, is unaware of there being two missions. It is therefore…

Just then Roger heard Admiral Welles' booming voice in the hallway, and was almost too taken aback by what he had just read to act fast, though he did. Closing the file completely, he quickly sat down in a chair on the opposite side of the room — his mind racing. The file in which the paper sat had been opened when he first came in, but now he had closed it. However, he rationalized that it was better to take the chance of the admiral having a perfect memory, and recalling the exact state of his disorganized desk, than for him to have found Roger alone in his office with the letter sitting face up in an open folder. At best, Roger thought, Welles would find the file on the top of his desk and think himself lucky he had closed it before he left. Roger had just enough time to cross his legs, lean back, and pretend to be staring out a window.

"Ah, Mr. Mathews, good morning," the admiral said coming into the office. He went straight to the desk, and Roger was glad to see him nonchalantly toss the two folders he was carrying on top of the file from which he just read. "I'm sorry to have kept you."

"No problem, Admiral Welles. It allowed me to further dry

my clothes." He forced a smile but his heart was racing so fast he was sure the admiral would see it beating through his suit.

"Ah, yes, the weather is a bit nastier this February," Welles said, pushing back the heavy velour curtain and peering out the window. He let the curtain drop back into place and walked back to the desk and sat down.

"Furthermore," Roger added, "the reports are for this weather pattern to continue, which will help our mission. It will keep things that much darker, and as Nazi crossing post guards seem ill disposed to standing outside in bad weather, it should keep Captain Westmore better protected." Roger could not believe that he was talking so calmly and covering himself so well, having just learned that he and his lover had been entirely duped into a mission of artifice, and whose end could only mean arrest and possible execution for Clive.

"Well, then, lucky for us," Welles said, reaching over his desk and pulling across a large envelope, which he handed to Roger. "Enclosed are all the documents you and Captain Westmore will need — falsified Nazi travel permits, faux Vichy government papers, false identification for the Captain, as well as fake merchant shipping documents that you will give the harbormaster at Pevensey."

"Thank you, sir." He took the envelope and placed it on top of his briefcase that sat on the chair next to him.

"And it's too bad the captain isn't here," Welles continued, "but you can tell him I wish the both of you much luck, and a safe return home. This mission is most important, and once again is of enormous value to Britain's very survival. And we're proud to have the two of you retrieving the last and final piece to the Enigma puzzle."

Roger couldn't believe he was hearing this whitewash after what he had just read. He could barely suppress his feeling of deep anger and resentment, and it was all he could do not to start yelling. Instead, he shook the admiral's hand, thanked him, slid the envelope into a side pocket of his case, and walked to the door. Halfway out of the admiral's office, Roger stopped and quickly turned around — he hoped the level of anger he felt could not be seen on his face or heard in his voice, but he had to test the situation.

"Admiral," he asked, "if we don't get the rotor, or it turns out to be fake, what then?"

"Well, Mr. Mathews, we would have to wait for an actual Rotor IV to show up. Until then, we fight on. Good day."

Roger's mind was in a total state of disorder as he walked down the grand staircase of the Admiralty Building. He found himself getting into a cab that he had no recollection of hailing. In a fog, he could hear himself giving the cabby his address, and sliding into the cab, simply stared at the back of the seat in front of him for the duration of ride. He felt cornered, and the frustration of feeling like a trapped animal was immense. When the taxi pulled up to the front of his apartment he threw some money to the cabby and jumped out. He ran up the stairs two at a time, opened his apartment door, and picked up the suitcase that he had packed earlier that morning. He needed to get the hell out of London — he was suffocating the longer he stayed in the city. He wanted to run to Clive, but at the same time he wanted to hop on the next plane to the United States and pretend none of this ever happened. His heart had sunk into his stomach, and it felt like it would remain there. He now understood the terror that mothers and young wives felt when there would be knock at the door and a young officer carrying a death-white envelope would be standing at the threshold — his fear was theirs, but in this case it wasn't his son or husband, it was his lover.

He hailed another cab, and during the ride, tried to keep every detail of what he read in the secret message in his head. Roger didn't even bother to stop by his office, but went straight to collect his authorized Embassy vehicle, a small black coup, and was soon on the road heading towards Buckinghamshire, and to the estate of Bletchley Park, where he knew he would find a safe haven in Alan.

Stephen lay on his stomach, his smooth back and buttocks rose and fell like the soft mountains of Massachusetts. They had finished making love, Roger was in the bathroom brushing his teeth and Stephen was paging through a magazine. They were in Roger's dorm room, on an early but warm April morning, and the opened windows allowed a gentle wind to play with the curtains.

"If we take tomorrow's 2:14 to New York City, we can see a play," Stephen half-shouted as he tapped a pencil to the magazine.

"Can't," Roger said, peering out from the bathroom door. "Remember, my mother is coming to visit, and her train comes in this afternoon." His head disappeared back into the bathroom. "She's been shopping in New York, and decided to make an excursion here to Washington," his voice echoed.

"Oh, then you mean I have to go to New York with Thomas, then," Stephen said, hoping this would make Roger jealous. "After all, he's usually free on weekends, you know."

"It's not going to work, Stephen," Roger's head once again rounded the corner from the bathroom. "I'm not getting jealous, and I wouldn't miss a visit from my mother for anything. So, maybe it would be best that you take Thomas with you, but let me remind you there's probably a terrifying reason why Thomas is always free on weekends."

"Damn," Stephen said in half joking defeat, and rolled out of bed.

Roger walked through Foggy Bottom to the Mall, and then up to the Capitol, then across to Union Station. When he got to the Capitol, he glanced at his watch and was happy to see that he'd made good time, and his mother's train would be in very soon, if not already. When Roger rounded the Capitol, he saw that there was a commotion of fire trucks sprawled out in front of the train station, and policemen ringed the massive structure, keeping people away. He quickly made his way to the crowd of people out front, and asked a stout, middle-aged officer what had happened. The officer told him that a train coming in from New York caught fire a few miles from the station, and it spread so quickly it engulfed two cars, killing twenty or more people. Roger ran past the officer, who called out for him to stop, but Roger wasn't listening, nor would he have stopped even if he had heard the officer's shouts.

"Please, God, no. Please God, no," he chanted as he made his way through the main concourse towards the back of the station to where the trains arrived and departed. He passed the Romanesque statues of ancient warriors that ringed the frieze of the grand concourse — their massive shields protecting them from whatever might be thrown their way. Images of his mother trying to escape a burning, moving train filled his head with horror, and part of him wanted to run in the opposite direction, but his feet ran on, following the fetid smell of heated metal and burnt wood. He looked at every woman's face as he ran, hoping that he'd see her amid the crowd, and not seeing his mother made him grow ever more terrified. He followed the furor of firemen to a train whose two end cars were gutted into blackened skeletons. Very little remained of anything that had once been inside.

"Oh, my God, no!" Roger said loudly. A fireman standing nearby came up to him.

"Son, are you looking for someone?" the older man asked.

"Is this the train from New York?" Roger was almost in tears.

"No," the fireman replied. "Close, though, this is the train from Newark."

"What did you say?" Roger said, spinning around and grabbing the man's heavy fire-coat, his hands smearing into the muddied paste that had amalgamated from the ash, soot, and water, and was now caking the crevices and folds of the fireman's coat.

"Newark, I said, this train is from Newark — Newark, New Jersey," the man uttered as he turned to look back at the burned out carriages. "What a pity. Some of 'em were children, too." But Roger didn't hear this, he had already turned and was walking back towards the station, only now he was crying. Crying in relief, or crying in anger, or crying in fear, he didn't care. He stopped and looked up through the stations roofless sphere, up into

the sky, so clear and spotless. He prayed that he'd never have to go through that type of terror ever again, and somewhere nearby a train whistle blew a mournful scream…

Roger was startled out of his reverie by a train speeding by in front of him, its whistle blaring. He was in the car at a train crossing, with little recollection of how he had gotten there. He was, however, in Buckinghamshire and not too far from Bletchley Park. He thought to himself that as he had made this trip many times before, and knew the way by heart, he must have driven there automatically. The crossing guardsman pulled a long rope attached to the red and white barrier pole, which bounced into the air, and which would have allowed Roger to cross the tracks and drive on, but Roger was lost in his thoughts, and so the guardsman put two fingers to his mouth and blew a whistle. Dragged out of his thoughts once again, Roger put the coupe into gear, and drove onward to Bletchley.

Showing his ID at the gate, he drove onto the familiar grounds, which gave him the slightest sense of security. He parked the car, walked to the plain-whitewashed door of the plain-whitewashed longhouse, and pushed it open. The short walk down the hallway seemed interminable, and he thought that he'd never get to Alan's office.

"My God, Roger, are you ill?" Alan asked, opening the door after hearing his friend knock.

"I don't know," was all he could get out as Alan pulled him into his office. Roger caught a glimpse of himself in a small mirror on the wall and could understand why Alan thought him sick — his face was ashen white, his hair was a mess, his tie undone and hanging down to his thighs. Alan quickly lifted some books and papers from a chair, and moved them to the floor to make room for Roger. When Roger looked comfortable, Alan kneeled on the floor in front of him, took his head in his hands, and gently stroked Roger's face.

"Roger, what is wrong?" Alan asked.

"They fucked us, Alan," Roger croaked, relieved to finally hear himself saying it out loud. "They fucked us. It was all a lie, the mission is a lie, the whole damn fucking thing is a lie."

"What are you talking about?" Alan asked innocently, and it immediately dawned on Roger that it was quite possible that Alan was in on the deception all along. It only made enough sense. Alan would have trained the Alpha team members on how to tell the difference between an artificial Rotor IV and one that was genuine, just like he showed Roger and Clive. Alan had to have been in on the secret all along. This realization surprised him, and his anger at Alan's betrayal was swift, as he pushed the kneeling Alan, who rolled heavily to the floor.

"Roger, what the devil is wrong with you?" Alan gasped, though his pride hurt more than his person. Both men stood up quickly and were now facing each other, though Alan was keeping his distance, and even took a step back to be out of Roger's reach.

"I know what you're doing," Roger said angrily. "I read all about it on Welles' desk. The Alpha and Beta teams, ours being a decoy mission, the covert secret messages to be retrieved by the Nazis so that Clive would get caught while someone else gets out of France with the real rotor. I can't believe you were part of this, Alan, I just can't believe it."

"Roger, I don't know what the bloody hell you're talking about, but you have to calm down, otherwise I can't help you." Seeing how serious Alan was, and because he really wanted to believe he was wrong about Alan's involvement in the deception, Roger took a breath, and held it a second before speaking.

"You know nothing of the two separate teams?"

"No, I don't know what you're talking about." Alan was relieved that Roger was at least talking rationally, but he was still concerned about this puzzling interrogation.

"But how do I know you're not lying to me right now?" Roger

asked incredulously.

"Oh, Roger, stop fucking around." It was Alan who was now getting mad, a rare occurrence, indeed. "I have no idea what you're talking about, and you sound like you need immediate psychiatric treatment." He reached for his desk, picked up the telephone receiver, and waved it threateningly.

"Look, just put the phone down, okay?" Roger said, realizing he probably did sound out of his mind, and that he'd have to approach this differently. "Okay, then, answer me this. In the past three weeks, have you shown anybody else how to tell the difference between an actual rotor and a fake one?"

There was a moment of silence as Alan thought about the question.

"Well, yes, come to think of it, I have." Alan put the phone down and then brought his hand to his chin thinking. "A young American — he had all the necessary documentation, and I called one of the top aides I know at the Admiralty to confirm the permission. He was with your Federal Bureau of Investigations, and explained that he needed this information to take back with him to the United States for a project they were working on. I don't receive these kinds of visits regularly, but it didn't seem out of the ordinary."

"Alan, can you remember the man's name?" Roger asked carefully.

"Why, I have it written down." He opened his desk drawer and removed a large pile of little notes. "Ah, here it is. He didn't give me a calling card or anything, it was just on the documentation, so I tried to remember his name and just wrote it down after he left. Let's see here, Charles Van Garten, maybe Van Garden."

Roger immediately recognized the name as the one on the paper he read in Welles' office. He looked at Alan and nodded, relieved that his close friend had not been in on the deception after all.

While Alan made them both a cup of tea on a small electric water-boiler, Roger stood by the window and explained the whole day. He told how he saw Clive off that morning at the train station, how he read the file on Welles' desk, and how he got to Bletchley Park without even remembering how he got there.

"Oh, you poor thing," Alan said, coming up behind Roger and putting his arms around him. Roger appreciated the contact; it was anchoring and calming. Roger turned around and gently kissed Alan on the cheek.

"Thank you for being my friend," Roger said, gently rolling his fingers down Alan's face, remembering the tender moments they had together. Then his head dropped onto Alan's shoulder, and he whispered, "I just don't know what to do, Alan."

"You must talk to Clive immediately. If we leave now, we can reach Pevensey by eight o'clock."

"Alan, there's no place for us to run. How do we get out of this, what do Clive and I do?"

"My dear, I think you'll feel better once you've talked to the Captain; he'll know what to do." Alan was trying hard to sound calm and reassuring. He knew that the only thing they could do was to get to Pevensey as fast as possible.

Roger placed Alan's primitive Enigma machine and radio receiver in the trunk of the car, snugly between their luggage.

"Is something wrong, Alan?" Roger asked, noticing that Alan was just standing by the car, totally lost in thought. Staring and thinking, his mouth moved silently as his genius worked out a solution to something that was perplexing him. He snapped out of his daze.

"Roger, I have to go back into the hut. I just remembered I've forgotten a certain piece to the Enigma that I may need." He left and returned a few minutes later with a small box, which he put next to the rest of the equipment before slamming the trunk closed. Roger was already in the car, waiting.

"Very well, then, let's go," Alan said cheerfully, sliding into the passenger seat. Roger shifted into gear and they were off.

Roger was glad to have Alan with him and that he wasn't carrying this burden alone. However, he still felt trapped and very scared. He loved Clive more than he could any man, and had resolved that if the impossible happened and there was a successful ending to their mission, he would seriously talk to Clive about a permanent situation. He would sacrifice his inheritance, his station in life, his career, all of it, if it meant that Clive would come home from this ill-fated mission and the two of them could be together. His heart still hadn't left his stomach since this morning — his world was crashing in around him, and there was nothing he could do to stop it.

"Alan," Roger said after they had been on the road a while, "is it possible the Embassy's Chief of Staff didn't know about this?" He felt he was grasping for answers that had no intention of reaching back.

"Roger, there's little reason to believe this was anything but a bilateral mission. Sadly, I'm sure that the entire plan was arranged by both sides. Remember, there's an American involved in the other mission, so obviously the Americans were more than likely involved from the beginning."

"And what about Jean Pierre Du Mont of the French Resistance?" Roger tested. "The memo I read in Welles' office said that he was being duped, too. I can't believe the French Resistance would do that to their own representative."

"Why not?" Alan answered, "You're being duped, are you not, and desperate times call for desperate measures. If the price was right, and apparently it was, the resistance would have no choice but to include Jean Pierre in those being, as you say, duped."

"I guess you're right," Roger said. "And because the French Resistance is also behind the plan, they're not just getting three truckloads of goods, but because of the other team, they're probably getting quite a bit more. We can assume that they are getting six truckloads — our three and three from the other team.

But, Alan, would they really risk the lives of the guide, and the guys who will be driving the trucks?"

"I don't know, Roger, I just don't know."

"What about the rotor that our team is supposed to get."

"A fake, I'm sure," Alan said matter-of-factly. "And if your story is accurate, it may have even been supplied to the French by the British government themselves."

"Why would they do that?" Roger asked.

"Because they are probably doing everything possible to ensure that they get to the rotor before the Nazis, even if it means fabricating an artificial rotor and putting it in France to throw them off."

The two men fell silent as they drove through the darkening countryside. The rain, though it was more like a fine mist, had not let up since morning, further darkening Roger's thoughts. It was one of the worst feelings he had ever experienced — a combination of anger, depression, guilt, and fear. His mind played every moment he and Clive had spent together since they first met, like the fit of hysterical laughter the two had experienced one Sunday afternoon over the most trivial thing, or the time Clive made him breakfast in bed. Roger wished Clive was with him now, because all he wanted to do was to be held, and have Clive whisper in his ear that everything would be okay. He wanted to tell Clive he loved him, and found himself increasing the pressure on the accelerator, despite the slick and muddy roads.

They arrived in Pevensey not too long after eight o'clock that evening. The little inn where they would all be staying was not difficult to find in the small fishing town. The two men quickly entered and were met by the innkeeper, who was expecting their arrival. He told them that Clive and his party were at the Brass Lion pub, a five-minute walk away.

"Roger," Alan said after they were back outside. "Go and talk to Clive yourself. I think it's something you need to do privately with him. I will unpack the car and get these things inside. My Enigma machine and equipment can't really be left alone."

Roger looked at his friend and nodded.

"He'll know what to do, Roger," Alan added in a calming voice, putting his hand on Roger's shoulder. "This will all work out."

"Yeah, right," Roger said, turning and walking down the sidewalk. After a few steps he stopped and turned around. "Alan?"

"Yes," his voice answered from the depths of the trunk.

"Nothing. Well, just thanks." Roger then turned, and made for the Brass Lion.

He walked quickly, and when he entered the pub, his eyes took a few seconds to adjust to the darkness. He found Clive sitting in a back booth with two men he assumed were the captain and first mate of the LST ship that was docked in the harbor. His heart dropped at the sight of his cheerful, handsome lover, laughing and joking with his friends, oblivious to the fact that his whole world had just gone upside down.

Clive turned and noticed Roger standing at the door, and the innocent smile that crossed his face sent an endearing stab of pain threw Roger's heart. For a quick second, Roger contemplated not telling Clive about their false mission, but he knew he'd have to. Clive said something to his colleagues, who turned and looked in Roger's direction. Clive motioned him to come over. With leaded feet, Roger dragged himself towards the table, a faux smile on his face. There was a lock of Clive's hair that was somewhat out of place, and it was all Roger could do not to reach over and gently push it back.

"Jim, Clark, this is my partner in crime, Roger Mathews," Clive offered. "Roger, this is Captain James Penn and First Mate

Clark Hunter."

"Gentlemen," Roger said through his smile. He was dubious of everyone he now met, and at this point he didn't know who was in on the deception, but he also didn't want to raise red flags.

"How was your meeting with the admiral?" Clive quietly asked, lifting a mug of dark lager to his lips. "And, where's the professor?"

"Well, Alan is at the inn, and you and I need to discuss my meeting with Welles," Roger said, pushing his inflection so that Clive might hear in his voice the need to talk immediately —and alone. Roger had calmed down to the point where he could function, and plan, and think, and this gave him some comfort. However, he was still gripped with a sense of pure terror at their predicament.

Clive's face became momentarily serious as he picked up on Roger's cue, but tactfully reverted back to a smile.

"Well, then, Roger, no time better than the present," he half laughed. "Gentlemen, as we've just about gone over all our plans, we'll next see each other later this evening at 23:00 hours at the wharf. Until then, have a good evening." He rose and grabbed his thick pea coat from a worn wooden hook that jutted from the wall near their table, and the two men headed for the door.

They walked silently out of the pub, Clive closely following Roger as they headed towards the inn.

"All right, what's wrong," Clive asked when they were far enough from the pub, and he was sure there was no one else in hearing range.

"I don't know how to tell you this," Roger urged, "or how to begin, but we have big problems, Clive. I can't tell you right here. Wait until we get to the car."

"Roger, what the devil is going on." Clive sounded frustrated.

"The car is just up ahead," Roger nodded forward, "in front

of the inn."

The two men walked through the falling mist. They finally reached the car, and were about to get in, when Roger realized that despite what Alan said earlier, it might be better for Alan to be in on this, too.

"Wait here. I'll be right back," Roger said, as he dashed up the short walkway and into the inn.

Clive tried to call after him, but it was too late. He lit a cigarette and leaned against the car, desperately wondering what could be wrong. Within a minute, Roger emerged with Alan, who was wrestling to get into an oversized pullover sweater he had brought with him.

"Get in," Roger instructed the other two, opening the door and sliding into the driver's seat.

Clive took the passenger's seat, and Alan jumped into the back, sitting in the middle so he could see both men.

Roger, now safe with Clive sitting next to him, needed a minute to collect himself. The past six hours had so terrorized him that he was afraid that if he started talking now, he might break down, which made the feeling even worse. Roger felt his hand being taken, and followed it with his eyes as Clive brought it to his own cheek. Roger gulped, took in a deep breath, and slowly related to Clive the day's events. Clive sat and listened to the entire story, asking a question here and there to clarify a point or event. Alan would occasionally comment, too, leaning his head into the front from the back seat. It didn't take long, because the facts spoke plainly. When Roger finished, the three men sat silently for a while, the quietness interrupted by a few passing cars and a group of half-drunken men heading home to angrily waiting wives.

"Except for this knowledge," Clive finally said after putting his thoughts in order, "nothing in our mission has changed."

He finished and waited for a response. It took a minute, because neither Roger nor Alan understood what Clive was getting at. But Roger had an idea, and he was hoping he was wrong. So, to clarify, he decided to add to Clive's statement in the opposite direction he thought Clive was going with this.

"And so, with this knowledge, the mission isn't a mission. It's a fake, a trap, a farce, and we have to find a way out."

"No, the mission is a mission. We've just been given the nasty side of it, that's all."

"Clive, what are you trying to say?" Roger asked in disbelief.

"I'm saying that we're still going on with our plan. It's a bum rap, as you Americans call it, but for the sake of getting the final rotor into British hands we cannot abandon our mission."

Roger turned his body so it completely faced Clive, no easy task in the driver seat of a small English car. He couldn't believe what he was hearing.

"Clive, if the Germans catch you, they will kill you." Roger couldn't have said it with any more adamancy. "I cannot sit back and let you do this. Alan, would you excuse us a minute, please?"

Alan didn't say a word, but opened the car door and slid out, gently closing it behind him. He walked to the inn's front door, reclined on one of the small benches that sat on either side of the entrance, and lit a cigarette.

"Damn it, Clive, I can't believe what I'm hearing," Roger snarled. "Don't I mean anything to you, or is our relationship a farce, too?"

"Roger," Clive attempted to speak, "you have to see…"

"No, *you* have to see," Roger barked. Now, he was just plain angry. He was mad at the British government, mad at the U.S. government, and now mad at Clive. It hurt him to no end to be mad at Clive, and that made him mad at himself. "I never thought I'd fall in love with someone as much as I love you, never, and then you come into my life. I've been worried that something might happen to you on this trip, and if it did, I don't know what I'd do. I couldn't bear the thought of you not coming back to me.

So, how do you think I feel knowing that my worst nightmare is coming true? I can't just sit here and watch you to this to yourself. So, are you coming with me? We'll find a place to run to; we'll just leave."

"Roger, darling," Clive started earnestly, but was cut off.

"Don't fucking darling me, Clive," Roger shouted. "Are you going to kill yourself or stay with me, what will it be?"

"Roger, you don't understand, I'm an officer, and I've been trained to—" but Roger cut him off again. This time his tone was one of acute resolve.

"Clive, if you go ahead with this, I promise you I'll never talk to you or see you again. Even if you went and somehow made it back alive, you can forget it — nothing, gone, zero. Do you understand me?"

"Roger, I have a duty to perform, you have to understand," Clive begged, but Roger was already opening the door.

"Clive, I love you, but I can't love you and let you go on this mission," Roger croaked, "so if you go, I can't love you."

Roger hesitated a moment at the open car door, somehow hoping that Clive would change his mind, but that didn't come, so he stood up, closed the door, and walked up the path to the inn.

"Move your things to my room, and let him have your room," Roger angrily said as he passed Alan and pushed through the door of the inn. He couldn't believe that he had fallen in love with a suicidal maniac. He walked up the carpeted stairway to the room he had hoped to share with Clive that night. He sat on the bed, thinking. His eyes fell on the phone on the bed stand, and he picked it up and tapped the receiver.

"Hello, yes, Roger Mathews, room number two, listen, how can I get some petrol for my car… is anything open?" While he waited for the reply, he noticed that the light from the small table next to him enlarged his shadow on the opposite wall, making it the size of a giant.

"It's not opened 'til tomorrow? And there's no other place I can go?" Roger was surprised. "Okay, thank you."

He flopped back onto the bed with his head on the pillow, and thought about the possibility of taking the train to London, but slowly he realized that he couldn't bolt — there was nothing he could do but stay and watch as Clive got on that landing ship later that evening, only to sail away from him. He caught his reflection in the small mirror on the back of the door. He looked older, he thought, and tired, and ugly. He hadn't felt like this since Stephen had broken things off with him several years before.

He lit a cigarette, waved out the match, and threw it on the floor. Roger thought about going with Clive — that if they were going to go down, they'd go down together. But, he was an American, and when the Nazis captured the two men — and they would most certainly be captured — it would bring the U.S. into the war. In that instant, Roger almost understood Clive's motivation for continuing with their ill-fated mission. Clive only wanted to do what he believed was right for his country. But that understanding quickly faded and weakened when it was placed next to the fact that not only England, but also the good old U.S.A was sending Clive to his end. At that moment, all patriotism flew out of the room's slightly opened window like the smoke from his cigarette.

"Fuck the U.S.A.," Roger said out loud. He put his face into his hands and wished he had never met Clive, but then quickly changed his mind. He loved the man, and it wasn't Clive's fault they were getting screwed… but it *was* Clive's choice to go on this suicide mission. He continued to stare at his reflection in the mirror, and wondered what Clive was thinking.

After the car door slammed, Clive lit a cigarette. A few seconds later, the car door opened, and he thought for a moment that it was Roger returning, but it was only Alan, who quietly slid into the driver's seat. The two men sat for a few minutes without speaking.

"There's a chance," Alan said, breaking the silence, "that they'd take you as a spy. You know, hold you for a trade for a Nazi spy or something."

"No, the Nazis have become ruthless and arrogant, and don't believe they have the need for bartering. You know, Professor, that if they're already aware of this mission, they probably also know what they intend to do with me when they catch me."

"Well, Captain, that's if they actually catch you. I mean, there's still the chance you'll get away."

"Well, if what Roger read is true, then they know exactly where I'll be and at approximately what time. They'll be waiting like wolves."

"Are you scared?" Alan asked innocently.

"No. I'm waiting until there's a Nazi bullet about to enter my skull before getting scared," Clive said with only a hint of sarcasm. And he wasn't afraid at this point, only hurt. Hurt by his government, hurt by the fact that Roger didn't understand that there was a duty here that had to be performed, hurt that he knew Roger himself was in pain.

Roger sat on the bed thinking for quite some time. He walked to the window and looked down upon the car in the street below. He could make out the occasional glow as Clive puffed on his cigarette. He hadn't felt this alone in months, maybe more. He could deal with being alone, he just couldn't deal with the idea of Clive being killed. His mind went to all of Clive's little endearments — that he never used the toothbrush rack, but always put his brush on the windowsill; the way he couldn't say 'hello' when he answered the phone, but said something like 'ayah'; that sometimes Clive's hair would curl in a way that no matter how much Roger tried to push it back, it would fall back into place. Roger's mind went to all of these things, and more — he missed Clive, and on this last night before the mission, all he had hoped for was to have him in his arms until it was time for him to go.

He put his cigarette out in the small ceramic ashtray on the bed stand and stretched out on the bed, hands clasped behind his head, staring at the ceiling. He began to think some more, but soon fell into an exhausted sleep, which proved to be the perfect panacea to escape the pain, anguish, and fear he had been through over the past day. He woke when he felt someone enter the room, and knew in seconds that it was Alan. Roger listened to him putter about the room, and after several minutes he felt Alan's face come to his ear.

"Time to wake up, Roger," he heard his friend whisper. "It's almost eleven o'clock, and time to go to the docks to see Clive off."

Despite everything he was feeling, Roger knew Alan was right, and that he'd have to go and see Clive one last time. He rolled over with a moan, and got out of bed.

CHAPTER IV: DESTINATION

The old man made it to the higher level on the cliff and looked out over the ocean; it had been their favorite spot. Whether the tear that ran down his leathered face was from the cold or from sadness he didn't know. He gently drew the cuff of his raincoat across his cheek, erasing any sign a tear had ever existed. It was late in the afternoon, but the bleak, gray sky darkened things so that the world looked like a black and white photograph. The crashing waves below sent a salty mist into the air that collected on everything.

February 28, 1941

The mist broke over the bow every time the landing ship crashed through a wave, collecting on Clive's slicker and running down in snake-like beads. He could see, in the dark distance, small lights from the city of Boulogne-Sur-Mer. He walked back to the middle of the ship, passed through a narrow door, and was in the craft's warm bridge, where he appreciated the protection from the elements. It wasn't a stormy night, just a choppy one, and the bridge was dimly lit with a single sconce that jutted from the back wall. It was the only visible device on the ship producing light— the others had been turned off when they got close enough to the French Coast to be seen. The ship's captain, Jim, was at the helm, steering the vessel to a point that would deliver them a mile or two north of Boulogne.

"We should be ashore in a half hour, captain," Jim said, leaning back and talking over his shoulder.

"Good. We'll need to warm the engines of the lorries, and prepare them for a quick unloading."

The captain looked over at his first mate and gave a nod. Immediately the man went to start the engines of the three trucks on the ship. Being this close to occupied France gave them a sense of professional seriousness that differed sharply to earlier that evening, when they were laughing and being chummy at the pub.

Clive walked towards the back of the bridge, and opened the door to a small room. Actually, it was more the size of a windowless closet, with a small table and a single light from above. Within, and sitting on a ridiculously small stool, was Alan, and his assemblage of electronic equipment on the table in front of him. He was making entries in a small notebook, and seemed oblivious to Clive's presence.

"Alan," Clive said, breaking the professor's concentration. "You wanted to know when we were about a half hour to shore, and that's now."

Because his mind was still on the last calculation he was thinking about, Alan looked bewildered, as if he didn't understand a word Clive was saying. Suddenly, Alan shook it off, and came to his faculties.

"Oh, thanks, Captain. I can now actually start the test," and with that he began a small inventory of the devices in front of him, arranging the settings on the Enigma Machine. He made affirmative sounds with each check, and Clive, now becoming somewhat interested, leaned against the doorjamb to watch. When Alan seemed satisfied everything was as it should be, he flicked a switch and several lights appeared on the machine. Alan sighed, looking upward in a show of divine gratitude. He then looked at his watch, quickly jotted down the time in his little notebook, and began tapping away at the typewriter-like keyboard on the Enigma machine. His face pained with concentration, he would occasionally glance back from the Enigma's keyboard to his notebook, and once again start typing.

"How long do you think your test will take," Clive asked, but there was no response. He waited a second, but then realized that Alan was far too engrossed in the task at hand to speak. Shrugging, he smiled and shook his head, gently closing the door behind him.

Clive wanted to have one last check of the trucks, and walked to the ship's open hold where the first mate and three other sailors were already untying the thick ropes that held the three trucks in place. Clive opened the door to the first truck, its engine purring quietly, and grabbed an old, battered suitcase that was sitting on the passenger seat. From the suitcase he pulled out a road map that he had looked at many times in the past few weeks. He had practically committed the map to memory, but wanted to reassure himself by reviewing the red lines that wended their way across it, and marked his future.

If what Roger and Alan said was true, and he had no doubt that it was, it would still be possible for him to play the decoy by leading the Nazi's away from the real mission, then at the last minute escape, and get back to the coast in time for the rendezvous. It had crossed his mind that in all likelihood, because his mission was a decoy, and that it was expected the Germans would capture him, there would be no rendezvous ship, and he'd be stuck in occupied France. However, he'd have to cross that bridge when he came to it.

From the suitcase, he also pulled out a gun holster, from which he drew his French-made M76. He could almost make out the reflection of the stars overhead in its polished black barrel, and its grip and trigger mechanism fit his hand like a calfskin glove. He released the lock, opened the chamber, and for the third time that day checked to make sure it was loaded before flicking it closed, sliding it back into the holster, and strapping it around his chest. The weight of the gun, and the light pressing of the holster on his side, always gave him a sense of security, and the fact that he was an award-winning marksman was comforting, too. Clive knew that if there were ever a time for greater precautions, it would be now. Although his two previous missions to France were less complicated, he was nonetheless stopped by the Nazis on the last, and lightly interrogated at a roadblock just outside Paris. If it weren't for excellently forged documents, and his ability to speak native French, he may not have been released.

Standing next to the idling truck, his mind turned to Roger, and how he looked a little while ago, when he, Roger, and Alan were standing on the dock watching the ship's crew load the trucks onto the landing ship. It was obvious to Clive that Roger looked sad, and was trying to keep up appearances because of the presence of the crew. He also noticed that when Roger spoke, it was only to Alan, or no one in particular, thus avoiding talking directly to Clive. He could understand Roger being upset, but hoped that on this occasion he would come around and say something, anything directly to him. After Alan and the crew were on the transport vessel, and it was time to leave, Clive walked over to where Roger was standing.

"I will do everything possible to come back to you," he said. Roger was looking at his feet, and Clive was afraid he wasn't going to say anything, but Roger slowly raised his head, his face now lit by a lamppost a few yards away. He looked back into Clive's face, slowly nodded twice and said, "You'd better." This was all the validation Clive needed, and he gently nodded back. The two men looked into each other's face one last time.

"I'll see you in a few days," Clive promised, as he turned and walked up the gangplank and stood next to Alan on the ship. As the boat pulled out into the harbor, he watched Roger standing on the dock by himself, and prayed that his promise could be kept.

The rest of the trip went quickly. He checked out all three lorries several times, walked around the deck to keep warm, and occasionally poked his head into the bridge to ask a question of the captain, or just to check on their progress. For the most part, though, he stayed on the bow of the ship, watching the coast of France get closer and closer. Usually, right before a mission, Clive liked to be alone with his thoughts.

"Captain Westmore?" Clive hadn't noticed the first mate walk up behind him. "It's time," was all the man needed to say.

Clive gazed into the distance, and figured by the looks of things they were only a quarter of a mile from the beach. "Please tell the captain I'll be up in a minute." The moment was here at last when he once again would go behind enemy lines. He never thought of himself as a spy, but never liked the idea of just being a sailor, either. And as much as he enjoyed the almost sexual excitement of penetrating enemy lines and stealthily eluding the Germans, he'd still rather be teaching at Oxford—if only the war were over. He couldn't wait until France was liberated, because he wanted to do some research on a dissertation he had been putting together, and which the war had put on hold. He had spent a lot of time in France in his youth, and every summer he, his brother, and his mother would idle the months of June through September in his mother's family home in Montpellier. Because French was also greatly used at home, his French was so native that even Frenchmen would try to guess where in France he was originally from. His mother educated him on all aspects of French culture, so that combined with his excellent language skills, his time spent in the country had given him a certain French *je nois se qua.*

By now, he was at the door to the ship's bridge. He turned to face the shore, and could barely make out the line of white that was the approaching beach, and upon which the vessel would soon land, ramming its front into the soft, fleshy sand.

"What do you say, captain," Clive asked, "we'll land in about five minutes, or so?"

"About that," was the reply. Clive walked back to the little room where Alan was performing his experiment. He opened the door to see Alan in the middle of packing up his equipment.

"All done, then?" Clive asked, leaning up against the doorjamb again.

"Yes, captain, I think it was successful, thanks," Alan said, smiling up at Clive.

"We're almost on the beach, and I have to get moving," he said gently. "You'll need to remain on the bridge, where it's safe and out of the way, and from where you can watch the landing."

"Clive," Alan started, and then stopped, noticing that even out of his navy uniform and dressed in ratty French-made civilian clothes he was a vision of masculine beauty. "Take care of yourself—make it back."

"Thank you, Alan," Clive responded. "I hope to see you in a few days." Clive turned and walked over to the helm where the captain was gazing through a pair of binoculars out the front windows of the bridge.

"Well, then, Jim," Clive said to the captain with a smile, reaching out and shaking his hand. "Once again, thank you."

"You take care, Clive," the man smiled back. "We'll see you in two days, right back here." Clive nodded, wondering if that were true, and went down to the front of the ship to await the landing.

Clive made his way to the cargo level, and slid into the first of the three lorries, its engine still quietly idling. He looked up and saw the first mate ready at the gate, which he would lower shortly after they touched land. In two minutes there was a sudden, dull lurch, as the ship drove into the sandy beach, and within seconds the first mate was pushing buttons and operating the gate's mechanisms. The gate finally dropped completely to the watery sand, and Clive gently drove the truck forward, onto the gangplank, and down several yards to where the gangplank met the beach. At about this point, the vehicle pitched forward and came to a stop as the front two wheels dropped over the brink and into six inches of water. Clive gunned the engine and felt the truck pitching forward, but the wet sand wouldn't release it. He gave it some more gas, but the angle of the truck seemed to make it want to push downward, further onto the sand.

"Fucking shit," Clive shouted as he hit the steering wheel in anger. He was just reaching for the door when movement caught his eyes on the beach in front of him, shadows moving quickly towards him. A feeling of cold, clammy fear washed over him as the three phantoms approached the truck. Clive wished he could use the headlights to see what was going on, but any headlights would be seen for even a mile or two up and down the beach, so he couldn't risk using them—everything would have to be done in the dark. He watched as two of the mysterious shadows went to either side of the front of the truck, and the third situated itself several yards in front. He thought he heard a woman's voice shouting an order, and all of a sudden the front of the truck was rocking up and down. Clive's moment of fear vanished as he realized he had just met his landing party.

"Come on, driver, move it off," he heard the voice, which was definitely that of a woman's, yelling. Clive accelerated, and with the rocking motion freeing the wheels, the truck lurched forward, and Clive drove the truck up the beach about twenty yards. He climbed out in time to see the second truck being rocked off the landing ship. It pulled up to where he was standing, and he could make out the form of a woman in the driver seat.

"You get the last one, and tell my men to hop on," she shouted through the truck's window. Clive ran back, passing the two men standing at the bottom of the gangplank. He ran towards the back of the LST, and slid into the driver's seat of the last truck. Looking up at the bridge, he could barely make out the frame of the captain and Alan, watching the process from their high perch. He gunned the engine and the truck moved forward to the end of the ramp, where it dropped the last few inches into the sand and once again became stuck. Clive made a mental note that if he ever got out of this alive, he'd make sure to mention this defect in his report. The two men on either side did their rocking, and in seconds the truck was free.

"Jump on," Clive yelled in French, and the two men grabbed hold of the sides and jumped onto the truck's running boards. He drove to where the other two trucks lay idling in the darkness, and turned around to see the landing ship, silhouetted against the white foam of the waves. The large heavy door was closing, and the vessel was already pulling itself out of the sand. He watched as the ship freed itself, and began moving backwards away from the beach.

The passenger door next to him opened, and the mysterious woman slid into the seat.

"Follow the truck there," she pointed. "Once we hit the road, we'll take the lead." It was too dark to be able to tell what she looked like, but her voice was wonderfully smoky. Clive found no need to respond, and slowly drove onward, following the truck in front of him. He glanced in the mirror to see the dark form of the third truck looming behind. They drove up the beach to where a small road began its steep incline up the side of the cliff. It was a perilous drive without lights, and a sharp hundred-foot drop to his left made Clive grip the steering wheel ever harder. When they got to the top, the headlights of the truck ahead flicked on, and Clive reached down to turn his on as well. If was nice finally having light, but he still could not see the features of the woman next to him. The truck ahead pulled over to the side to let them take the lead.

"I am Captain Clive Westmore," Clive finally said, "and you must be my guide. I have to admit, I was expecting you to be a man."

"I'm sorry to have disappointed you," she replied somewhat coldly. "I am Claudette, and yes, I am your guide."

"Oh, no, don't get me wrong. I was only saying I was surprised, not that I doubted your ability. It's just that when Jean Pierre described our guide as being the best and the bravest, I naturally assumed that, well, that you'd be a man."

"Jean actually said the best and bravest," the voice now asked, slightly entertained. "Ha! My brother is such a flatterer."

"Jean Pierre is your brother," Clive asked.

"Yes, I am Claudette Du Mont, his older sister by three years."

"I see, then," his mind racing to the conclusion that Pierre certainly did not know about the duplicity of the mission, or why else would he risk the life of his own sister.

"Your brother is quite the businessman."

"Yes, he has always been able to manage things. I have taught him well," she said with little inflection, and Clive wasn't sure whether she was joking or serious.

"We follow this road straight into Abbeville," she explained, "and the driver of the first truck, René, will take the lead and we'll follow him to the drop off point. Then we'll head to Amiens."

"You'll have to excuse me, but it's been a few months since I've been on the continent, what are the checkpoints like," he asked in the same tone one would ask about the weather.

"They're now usually found just before going into most of the larger towns," she responded. "Sometimes across certain bridges, too. It is now eleven-twenty, and we should be able to make it to Abbeville by one o'clock."

She waited a few seconds before speaking again. "So tell me, captain, I was already aware that your French was good, but I didn't know it was this good. Why?"

"My mother is from Montpellier, and I was brought up speaking both French and English."

"And what was her family name?"

"It's an old name, actually, d'Auberive," Clive responded with a flourish.

"It certainly sounds like an aristocratic name."

"It's been in the area for centuries, and owes its significance to a great great-grandfather who served under Napoleon," Clive said. He was hoping that the lonely road would produce a headlight from which he could see her face, and no sooner had he thought that did he got his wish, as a headlight zoomed from around a sharp turn and illuminated the inside of the truck's cab. Clive glanced her way; she was young, about twenty-six, and her lips were thin and intelligent. Her nose, although not small, was well proportioned and rested between two beautifully high cheekbones. Her hair color was hard to distinguish because it was tied up with a kerchief, but he assumed a dark blond to brown. Nevertheless, in the moment of the passing headlight, Clive was given the picture of wholesome beauty, but one that also held a deep inner strength.

"You're not wearing a beret, or dressed like the men," Clive noticed. He'd seen other women of the French Resistance dressed this way, and always thought it looked silly.

"Women who want to be like boys, ha!" she said. "They think by dressing like men that they can to manly things, and that expelling the Germans can only be done by men, and so they feel the need to look like men, and so…"

"We've got a problem," Clive interrupted, having just noticed that the last truck had fallen behind and was flicking his lights in a mad attempt to get their attention. He slowed the truck down looking for a place to turn around.

"Probably the engine, maybe a flat," Claudette guessed, leaning forward and looking in the side view mirror. Clive found a wide space in the road to turn the truck around, and within a minute they were all standing around the back of the lorry looking at a very flat tire.

"Well, messieurs," Clive said, rolling up his sleeves, "let's try to have this done in half an hour, shall we."

"Monsieur, you sit down and rest," one of the men said. "You have a long trip ahead of you still, we can manage this."

"He is right," Claudette chimed in. "We will be driving all night, so this is a good opportunity to stretch your legs."

Clive walked over and sat on a large rock to the side of the road and watched the men work—Claudette stood above them.

They had just left Roger's apartment and were on their way to the Admiralty for a meeting with Admiral Welles. He and Roger had just kissed in the back of a cab during daylight hours, breaking a taboo that both, up to now, had adhered to. Despite the fact that cabs were very roomy, and passengers sat so far back it was almost impossible for the cabbie to see them, the risk of being noticed was too great, and woe to Clive and Roger should anyone see it and report it. Roger was always the one more worried about being seen, though Clive wasn't too anxious to be caught either.

He and Roger both had shared tales of school chums who were abused by other children for being somewhat lispy, fair, and delicate, and who were, for all intents and purposes, homosexual. Clive and Roger had even talked about how difficult it was to stand by and do nothing as their closest friends tormented those young boys who were known to be intimate with other young boys. Their peers weren't their only tormentors, though, as teachers and school administrators also took part in this, and constantly emitted subliminal reminders to students that two boys touching in anyway other than in sport was an aberration. Clive well understood what it felt like to long for the physical closeness of certain classmates—to brush gently against them as he'd walk beside them to class, or walk back from the rugby pitch with his arm around their shoulder. However, with societal signals all around that forbade such longings, and his position as the son of an English lord, he could not act upon his true urges, and so whiled away his school days in denial and distant love. It pained Clive to no end when, throughout his school years, he found a kindred spirit, but with no possible hope of getting close and forming a relationship. He noticed when he got to university that being different drove men in two distinct directions; for some it drove them deeper into work and study, as it did with Alan, and others it drove deeper into sport and masculinity, and the need to prove themselves above the rest, as it did for Clive and Roger.

"Don't look so annoyed," Clive said quietly so that the driver would not hear. "No one saw a thing, not even the cabby."

"It doesn't matter," Roger responded sternly. "All it would take would be for someone to see it, jot down the cab number, and file a complaint with the local constabulary. There are laws, Clive, that make it punishable to do such things, both in public, and in private."

"I have been a subject of this country all my life," Clive said, sounding very serious, "and I'm perfectly aware of the fucking laws about it, thank you very much." They sat in silence for a moment.

"Furthermore," Clive began again, leaning close to Roger's ear, "if you don't want to get fucking caught, don't kiss back." Clive moved back to his side of the cab and stared out the window, arms folded over his chest.

"I can't," Roger said after a moment of thought. Both men contemplated this for a second, and then looked at each other, their handsome faces glaring. Clive was the first to smile, and then Roger. Still grinning, Clive leaned back and continued looking out the window.

✿   ✿   ✿

Somebody was tapping his shoulder—it was Alan, returning from taking part in getting Clive to France and running his Enigma experiment. Roger had drifted into sleep in the chair in his room not too long after returning from the wharf to see Clive off.

"What time is it," Roger asked, rubbing his eyes.

"It's shortly after one o'clock in the morning," Alan replied groggily, as he slumped onto the bed. He slid off his shoes, and they fell to the floor in two resounding clunks.

"But wait," Roger implored, "you can't fall asleep yet. You have to tell me how the crossing went."

"Oh, Roger, I ever so need sleep. Clive is there safe and sound, there was virtually no problem with the landing, and looking at the time, he's probably already made the first drop off in Abbeville."

"And your experiment, how did that go?"

"I don't know, Roger," Alan said, half asleep. "As with most experiments, sometimes you just have to wait for the results."

"It's the waiting that I can't stand. What time did you guys land on the beach? Alan? Alan?" but Alan was no longer awake, and all Roger heard was the slow and quiet breathing of a sleeping man.

✧   ✧   ✧

The flat tire had cost them a full hour, and they didn't reach Abbeville until two o'clock in the morning. They drove into town, and the two other trucks pulled to the side of the road. Clive, following Claudette's directions, immediately turned down a dead-end street not too far from where the other trucks had stopped. The neighborhood was deserted and rundown, and they pulled up in front of a darkened house that sat at the end of the block. They were certainly expected, because they barely had a chance to open their doors when three men came out of a side door.

"Good morning, Claudette," a cheerful young voice said. From the headlights bouncing of the house, Clive could make out the form of a young man who couldn't have been more than twenty.

"Hello, Tomas," she responded. "We're sorry we are late, but we had a flat tire."

"No problem. It's not like we had a concert to go to or anything."

"Funny," Claudette shot back. "Tomas, this is Captain Clive Westmore of the Royal Navy—Clive, this is Tomas Quentin of the French Resistance." The two men shook hands, each nodding to the other with a smile. By this time, the two other men had already slid into the truck, and were backing it into a large barn that sat to the side of the house.

"How are the roads to Amiens," she inquired, and for an instant Clive, his mind still on the flat tire, thought she meant driving-wise.

"You should have no problem," said the young man. "A week ago orders came from Resistance Leadership to keep the roads between the towns you'll be traveling clear of subversive activities, so as not to draw more troops."

"Good. We must be going. We're already running behind schedule, and need to make up for lost time."

"You two have a safe trip," Tomas said with a wave, not losing his cheerfulness.

"Do tell your mother I said hello." She and Clive had already turned and were walking down the street towards where the other two trucks were parked and waiting for them.

Their trip to Amiens was uneventful, but upon entering the small city, they were stopped by a young Nazi SS soldier standing in front of a makeshift crossing gate. Clive showed him their forged papers, offered the young man a cigarette, and was allowed to pass. Once they entered the town, things went just as smooth as the first drop-off, almost frighteningly so. They pulled up in front of a darkened house in a remote part of the city. Two men, an older one wearing a tunic, and a younger man dressed in black came out of the house. With them was a woman. Clive noticed that she was wearing pants, a shirt, and the quintessential beret on her head. A cigarette dangling from her mouth, Clive thought, would have completed the scene.

"You're late," the woman said with a tinge of annoyance.

"We had a flat tire," Claudette replied, "and hello to you, too, Brigita."

"I'm sorry," the woman said, "it's just we had planned to start distributing this equipment today, and now we're thrown off our schedule."

"Well, with three trucks and a distance to go, it would have been best had you considered the possibility that we might run into trouble."

"Maybe you should have worked that into your schedule, and given us a window of time in which you'd be here."

"That will be enough, Brigita," the older of the two men standing with them said. The Brigita woman crossed her arms in front of her chest and sulked.

"I'm sorry, but Brigita is very dedicated. I am Alban, it is a pleasure meeting you," he said, reaching and shaking Clive's hand.

"Likewise," Clive responded.

"Thank you, Claudette, for delivering this equipment and supplies to us, we've certainly needed it."

"It is my pleasure, Alban." As the engine of the truck they were standing next to started up, the headlights went on, and the three realized that Brigita and the other man had disappeared into the truck. They took a step back, as it pulled onto the street, and watched it turn the corner and disappear.

"Well, as we're already late, we must be on our way," Claudette said, reaching out and shaking the man's hand.

"Yes, Godspeed, my child."

"It was a pleasure meeting you," Clive said, to which the man bowed his head regally.

They walked back to the last of the three trucks, their mission two thirds accomplished. It almost seemed too easy, and Clive wondered if he wasn't, in fact, headed into a trap. The trap didn't materialize in Amiens, and Clive sighed a low deep breath as they left the small city. The same young officer who they encountered upon their arrival stopped them briefly once again, but he recognized them and waved them through without even questioning the fact they entered with two trucks, but were leaving with one.

Now it was just Clive and Claudette, driving on a craggy road that was so full of mud and tank tread marks that it was obvious there must have recently been a major passage of the Warmacht. The moon was now rising, and the clouds gave way to a dark purple sky, spotted with gleaming stars. They drove through ancient small towns and groves of apple trees, vineyards that went on for miles, and wooded areas not unlike those Clive played in when he was a child in Montpellier. They were on their way to Arras, and because of the road's treacherous condition, Clive was praying they didn't get another flat tire.

"Do you still have family there," Claudette asked him as they bounced around in the cab.

"Hmmm? Oh, in Montpellier? Yes, we occasionally get news from them. I have an aunt and uncle, and several cousins."

"That is good," she said.

"So, how did you come to join the great French Resistance."

Claudette was looking out the window as they passed a burned and bombed out farmhouse and barn, barely lit by the cold moon that hung in the sky. The building was a reminder that even from the very beginning, the Nazis met resistance from brave individuals who refused to give them the ease of taking their land without a fight.

"Why did I join the Resistance," she repeated. "As with most things that deeply change people's lives, there was one terrifying incident that compelled me to join the Resistance, and which I still have nightmares about…"

The Nazis were coming towards their town, and she was trying to get home the fastest way possible. She was very scared, and frightened by the occasional rat-a-tat of machine gun fire and occasional explosion. That's why she decided to take a shortcut through the vineyard of Monsieur Tanebre, who had been telling townspeople for weeks that if the Germans came, he and his sons would show them what he called "Napoleonic spirit." Claudette's shortcut would carry her past the Tanebre farm, and this made her a little nervous, not knowing what she'd find.

She smelled the smoke even before she took sight of the farmstead. Walking over the hill, and looking down upon the sad scene, she was amazed at the chaos. The ancient barn was completely on fire, with tongues of flame leaping fifty feet into the air. Claudette hoped to herself that the two cows and new calf had somehow gotten out, but she doubted it. She continued walking down the hill, terrified that she might meet up with Nazi soldiers, but she saw no one, not at least until she was halfway down the hill, at which point that she began making out their bodies.

She could count all four, lying in the farm's puddled yard. The gruesome sight made her want to turn her head, but she couldn't—the sound of machinegun fire was getting closer behind her. As she neared the first two bodies, which were lying next to each other, their hands almost touching, she saw Maurice and Stephan. Maurice's lower leg had disappeared into a puddle whose rainwater had turned red. Stephan's smooth brown hair was matted and muddied, his dead eyes staring at his brother. She had to look away, and slowly brought her hands to either side of her head, somehow hoping she could wrench the gruesome sight from her mind. A bomb blast, no more than a mile away, forced her to move on, and she headed towards the farmhouse, where the other two bodies lay several yards apart. One was

Monsieur Tanebre lying on his back, his stomach ripped open like a recently butchered pig. Claudette quickly turned away, looking upwards towards the sun, staring at it so that it would blind her and she'd not have to see that sight again. She took a breath, and let her gaze fall on the small body that rested a few yards away, and could only have been eleven-year-old Jean. He had fallen with his head against a small tree, his eyes closed in deathly slumber. A rifle, which seemed almost taller than the boy, had fallen next to him, which further lent to the image of a boy who had fallen asleep while out shooting quail. She stooped down and looked at him more closely, gently moving a wave of hair from the dead boy's face, and then stroking his smooth, hairless cheek. He had been a very sweet boy, with whom she had spoken to many times, and she remembered that he had wanted to be a doctor when he grew up.

Suddenly, she became angry, very angry. Not the explosive type of anger, but the festering, righteous type, which burns and cauterizes painful things into personal causes and objectives. She picked up the rifle that lay next to the boy and headed home…

"…and since that day, I've been in the Resistance," she finished, leaving Clive speechless for a moment.

"That must have been most terrifying for you."

"It was, but although the terror is gone, the memory forces me to carry on. Worse, still, I have seen similar sights since joining the Resistance, but these spur me on even more. Ah, we are almost there," she finished, as they passed a sign that indicated they were entering the city of Arras. Clive looked at his watch, from which he could barely make out the time of four-thirty. They were running over an hour late, which would give them just enough time to get to the small city, make the drop-off, and go into hiding before the sun rose—cutting it far too close for Clive's comfort.

"We will have to pass through a checkpoint," Claudette said, sounding very serious. "It usually has the same two men, and both take turns leaving for hours with a few of the local women. I have arranged for one of the soldiers to be well occupied by a young girl named Chloe, who will keep him busy until about six this morning," she was smiling slightly as she said this. "This leaves us dealing with only the one officer."

"And this happens a lot, here?" Clive asked.

"It happens enough. These are just conscripts, even their sergeant is aware of their arrangement."

"I'm glad to see you have things so well planned," Clive said, nodding his head. "I'm further glad you hadn't arranged it to be a shorter romp, our flat tire used up quite a bit of time, and we lost more than we thought."

"Chloe is good at what she does," Claudette laughed slightly. "Here it is now," as they rounded a corner and came into sight of the makeshift gatehouse. Clive steered the truck up to the closed gate and stopped. To their surprise, however, not one but two figures came out and approached the truck.

"Something's gone wrong," Claudette said quietly.

"This isn't good."

As the soldiers walked to each side of the truck, Clive instinctively put his hand to his side, making sure his gun was in his pocket. The visors on their hats shadowed their faces, and all that could be seen were their lower jaws, which gave them an ominous appearance. The shorter soldier seemed to be the higher ranking of the two, probably an Untersharführer, Clive thought, noticing the insignia on his mousy gray uniform, and because the taller soldier seemed to be trying to keep a step behind as they walked. The buttons that ran down their coats glimmered in the cold light of the single light bulb that hung from its wire on a pole, and each had their Karabiner-98 rifle swung over their shoulders.

"Good evening, and where might you be going," the higher-ranking soldier asked in very good French, leaning in towards Clive in the driver's seat.

"We are delivering bread," Clive said, thinking the question rather stupid seeing that they were driving a bread delivery truck. He nonetheless offered the soldier the forged paperwork and bill of laden, but they were ignored.

"Ah, I see. Well, let's take a look in the back, shall we," the Nazi asked, opening Clive's door, while at the same time Claudette's was opened by the other soldier. Clive and Claudette got out and followed the men to the back, the officer talking as they walked.

"We have had an excessive amount of Resistance activity in this area, and so we can't be too careful, now, can we."

"We understand," Clive said, making sure his French was at its best.

"As a matter of fact, you probably would not have gotten into town at all had you come earlier," the soldier said in a chatty tone, making it obvious that he had been stationed here long enough to believe it was safe to converse with the locals. "We had a large contingent of SS officers come into town earlier today, taking over all of the checkpoints and setting up a small headquarters in one of the hotels. They seemed to be looking for some Resistance members or something, and they were stopping every vehicle that came or went. But then this morning at about two o'clock they very quickly left town as if they had a train to catch or something."

"That is a surprise," Clive said, trying to sound conversational. He knew this detachment could only have been there to intercept him and the rotor, but now he was very confused, because if they were here to finally trap him, why weren't they still here—what made them leave town so quickly? It at least explained why both soldiers were here tonight instead of just the one, because after the group of SS officers came into town, these soldiers were most likely thrown off by it, and didn't want to risk anything. That was why the one soldier didn't go off with Claudette's friend.

"Yes, this is a rare occurrence," the Nazi said. He walked to within a few paces of the back of the truck, swung his rifle off his shoulder and to his chest, and pointed it towards the truck's two back doors. "Please stand back," he said, giving a nod to the other soldier, who walked over and started untying the leather straps that held the doors closed. He untied the straps and quickly flung the doors open—nothing was inside but the bread. The officer swung the rifle back to his shoulder, and both men quickly fished in their pockets for small flashlights, which they shined into the back of the truck.

The shafts of light cast shadows on hundreds of loaves of bread. What they were actually seeing was the cut off ends of bread, which were ingeniously hiding the rifles, ammunition, and other supplies in makeshift bins behind them.

"Get up and take a look," the shorter Nazi said to the taller one in German. Clive understood some German, but it was not his language of choice, and he didn't speak it very well. The taller man climbed on board, and lifted the sacks of bread that sat on the floor and felt through them. These were filled with whole loaves of bread that had been baked with extra yeast so that the trucks would smell like fresh bread. Clive held his breath, because if the German soldier tried to pull out any of the fake pieces of bread, he would easily see the deception, and all would be lost.

"It looks fine to me," the soldier said. As he took a step towards the open doors, though, his foot caught on one of the sack's drawstrings and he tripped. Falling forward, he flailed his arms and fell to the floor, but not before breaking several pieces of the faux bread off the wall, exposing the wire mesh that had been holding them in place. Clive automatically put his hand in his pocket, and wrapped it around his pistol, waiting for the inevitable.

"What is this," the soldier said, sitting on the floor of the truck, holding a piece of broken bread in each hand. Suddenly Clive and Claudette heard the sound of the safety being unlocked on the rifle behind them. Instantly, Clive pivoted on his heels, drawing the gun from his pocket. His mind was working so fast that he wasn't even sure he was going to shoot the Nazi, but by the time his gun was brought level with his chest, he knew there was nothing else he could do. As the officer was finishing bringing his rifle up, Clive fired a single shot, and a small area of the man's uniform seemed to explode as the bullet pierced his chest, killing him almost instantly, hurling him backwards to the ground.

"Clive!" Claudette shouted. He immediately knew by the direction she was looking that he needed to quickly turn and get off another round at the soldier in the truck. As he pivoted, he instantly saw that he'd have to aim and shoot fast, because the second soldier already had his side pistol coming up to fire. Clive pulled the trigger, and felt the backlash of his gun as the soldier on the truck looked stunned, the bullet having grazed his left arm. The Nazi then fired his gun, which was probably more a reflex from having been shot, the bullet entering the earth near Claudette's feet. Clive fired again, the bullet this time finding its mark, and the Nazi soldier crumpled to the floor amidst the crumbs and pieces of broken bread.

"We need to move fast. Quickly, get his arms," Claudette said, picking up the feet of the soldier on the ground. Clive obeyed, hurrying over and grabbing the man from under his shoulders. They carried him to the truck, and put him in lying next to the other dead soldier. She produced a small flashlight, and examined the ground where the man had died. "Good," she said, "no blood." Clive was impressed as he watch Claudette walk around picking up spent casings. She stood for a second, counted out loud as she fingered each, and slid them into her pocket, satisfied that she had them all.

"Get my bag from the truck, please," she said matter-of-factly. Clive walked over, reached in, and grabbed the small carpetbag Claudette had been carrying. By the time he reached her, she was already standing at the guardhouse. He handed her the bag, and she reached in, producing a bottle of perfume, then proceeded to dab her finger with the perfume, and touch things throughout the small room—the chair, a paper or two on the desk, the collar of one of the coats hanging on a rack. Within a minute, the place smelled strongly of rosehips and honeysuckle. Claudette then produced a tube of lipstick, which she bent down and rested at the foot of the desk where it would first go unnoticed, but would inevitably be found if someone were searching the whole room.

She walked to the door where Clive was standing and turned around to look at the room.

"Tisk, tisk," Claudette said amusingly. "They've run off with their girlfriends, and have left their post."

"How capricious," Clive mocked, turning and walking back to the truck. He closed the two back doors on the dead men, tying it back with the leather cord. They climbed into the truck, and drove on; the sky in the east was getting brighter.

"We'll be there in ten minutes," Claudette said, noticing that Clive was looking towards the brightening east.

The sky was pink with the rising sun, but the water he was staring into shimmered black and cold. Roger couldn't sleep, so he had dressed and left the inn to go for a walk. He now found himself standing on the pier in the same place he'd stood the night before, when he was trying to be strong and emotionless so Clive wouldn't see how much pain he was in, or how horrible he felt about what happened and how he had reacted. Maybe he had made a mistake—Clive deserved to be heading out on a mission like this with the two of them on better terms. Now, standing on the pier with the sun bouncing off the gray waters, the sailors and docks men already at work around him, he wished he had spoken to Clive differently, told him that he loved him, and that he wanted nothing more than Clive to come back to him. Even though they both knew that under the given circumstances, this was not going to be the case. A tear ran down his smooth face, whether from the cold or from sadness, he didn't know. He glided the cuff of his raincoat gently over his cheek, erasing any sign a tear had ever existed. He stood and watched one of the ships chug through the small harbor until it disappeared around a corner, and he could only see the top of the ship gliding along the tops of the trees. He heard the sound of the dock's planks giving way to heavy footsteps, which he assumed were just some sailors passing him on the way to their ship, but the footsteps didn't pass by, and he followed them with his ears until he heard whoever these people were come up right behind him.

He turned to see three U.S. Military Policemen standing right in front of him. All three were in amazing physical shape, even for MPs, and through their uniforms, Roger could see they were muscular, and built like Clive.

"Mr. Roger Mathews," the leading man asked.

"Yes," Roger replied, "that's me."

"You're to come with us," the man said, as the other two moved to either side of Roger.

"What is this, where are we going?" Roger asked in alarm.

"We were instructed to simply get you and bring you, we were not told why," the officer responded calmly as they started walking off the pier towards the street. Was he being arrested? Did they find out that he knew about their mission being a decoy? Did they find out about he and Clive? Or worse, are they bringing him in to tell him that Clive was caught by the Nazis? Either way, he was terrified, and convinced nothing good was about to happen.

When they reached the road, waiting for them were two large Rolls Royce limousines. Roger noticed they were both Wraith models, slender and elegant, their curtains drawn closed for privacy, and both as black as the water he had been peering into just moments before. One of the men walked to the door of the first limo, opened it, and motioned for Roger to get in. He was nervous, and could see nothing within the dark confines of the car. The man motioned again for him to get in. Roger hesitated a second more, and then bent down and slowly entered the vehicle. It took a moment for his eyes to get accustomed to the dimness inside the car, and he was surprised at what he saw. Sitting on the seat directly behind the driver was Admiral Welles, and his personal assistant sitting next to him with a notepad on her lap. Next to her was FBI Agent Pomboi, looking somber and serious as usual, maybe more so now. On the back seat, though, and facing Welles, was Alan, who looked at Roger and gave a shrug, suggesting that he, too, had no idea what was going on.

"Come in, Mr. Mathews," Admiral Welles said, waving his large, beefy hand in the direction of the space next to Alan. Roger slid in, and said nothing. He still didn't know what was going on, and he was still very scared. The car door closed and Pomboi tapped on the glass behind him, suddenly the car started moving. Roger turned and saw that the other Wraith was following them, and probably contained the three well-built MPs.

"Mister Mathews, Professor Turing, I don't know where to start," Admiral Welles began. "Let me first say that as far as we know, Captain Westmore is still safe, and presently in Arras. But, we need to tell you something about your mission." Roger was so elated to hear that Clive was safe that he almost didn't hear what Agent Pomboi said next.

"We don't have the time to be gentle, Mr. Matthews, and so basically let me tell you that there were, in fact, two missions to get this rotor, yours and another group."

"Your team, Roger" the admiral interjected, "had been designated a decoy mission and things were set up so that Clive would receive a decoy rotor in order to throw the Germans off the trail of the team that was actually getting Rotor IV. In other words, we were hoping the Nazis would go after Captain Westmore, and draw attention and heavily needed manpower away from his counterpart and who was to retrieve the actual rotor."

"We also sent deceptive messages to the Nazis about your plan," Pomboi informed them, "steering them to Arras, and giving them the route that Clive was using to enter the city."

"So, the American government was in on this from the start?" Roger asked Pomboi directly, seeking confirmation, remembering quite well that the letter he saw on the admiral's desk was addressed to agent Pomboi.

"We agreed to take part," Pomboi explained tersely, "as long as there was no possibility that the Germans could link the United States to the mission. We are not yet at war with Germany, and so need to be careful about how and when we do enter this conflict."

"Did the other team know about us?" Roger asked.

"That's a good question, Mr. Mathews," answered the admiral, "but the answer would be no, they did not know. We wanted both teams to work fully independent and with no knowledge of the other. I'll be honest with you, however, in saying that the only other party who knew that there were two teams was the French Resistance itself."

"Did our contact, Pierre Du Mont, know too?" asked Roger.

"No, the French Resistance kept that from him at our request. They were getting six lorries loaded with weapons and supplies, and so agreed to keep Mr. Du Mont in the dark, too. This, again, so that we could keep the integrity of each mission separate."

"Integrity," Alan blurted sarcastically. "So, what you're saying is that you were willing to sacrifice the life of a captain of His Majesty's navy to obtain this rotor."

"Doctor Turing," the admiral responded, "our people are dying daily. Innocent men, women, and children in cities being bombed, soldiers who die and perish in the African sands, and just as importantly right now, our merchant mariners. These men who sail the ships that bring us food, supplies, ammunition, and military equipment, the very things we need to outlast this war, are being drowned daily. And as they drown, their precious cargoes sink with them. These people are all being sacrificed, doctor, and for many of them, like the innocents in the cities, there is no tangible thing like a rotor that they're dying for."

"But, admiral," Alan continued, "the moral dilemma here is that you actually put this man in harm's way, and misled him to be put there."

"Doctor Turing, Mister Mathews, we don't have time to go into questions of ethics," Pomboi hissed. "The truth of the matter is that what was once the decoy is now the actual mission, and we're desperately scrambling to get the real rotor to intercept with Captain Westmore."

"Wait…" Roger leaned forward towards Pomboi, so close that he could smell the stale odor of cigarettes on Pomboi's clothes. "What are you saying?"

"Similar to yours," the admiral began, "the actual mission was ferrying three trucks of supplies and ammunition for a trade with the French Resistance. It was crossing the Channel from Dover, when for some reason, we don't know why at this point, their LST landing vessel capsized and sank."

"Oh, my dear," Alan breathed aloud.

"What happened to the crew," Roger asked.

"Fortunately, all hands were rescued. They had enough time to use their wireless to inform us of what was happening—that they were listing badly, and taking on water. They only landed ashore within the last hour or so."

"Agent Pomboi," Roger said, "What did you mean by trying to have the real rotor intercept with Clive." Just then, however, the car slowed and came to a stop. Roger looked out the window and saw that they were at a small airport—there was a single hanger, around which sat spitfires and other aircraft.

"The admiral will explain everything to you in good time," Pomboi said as the door next to him opened. "I have important business that I'm being called away on, and therefore won't be able to continue along. You, Mr. Mathews, are an important player at this point, and you must go with the admiral and give him any assistance you can. Be aware, though, that I will be following matters while I'm away, and that the U.S. government is also working hard to see this mission completed successfully." At that, Pomboi stepped out of the car, and walked towards the hanger, followed by the three handsome and well-built MPs. Roger noticed, however, that they were no longer dressed as Military Police, but now seemed to be wearing the uniforms of U.S. Air Force captains, which he thought odd. The door closed and the car began to drive away. Although he still had many questions, Roger would wait until they got to their destination. Until then, he watched the coastal scenery pass by as he thought about Clive, and how things had turned around so quickly. It wasn't too long before the car once again came to a stop.

They had pulled into a long driveway that led up to a small cottage overlooking the sea, and which sat high atop a cliff. Two guards were stationed at the bottom of the driveway, and recognizing the Admiral's car, let it pass with a salute. The limo stopped near the cottage, and Roger noticed that it looked as if it hadn't been lived in for quite some time—weeds had well overtaken the garden and path, and the shutters on the windows looked as if they had only recently been torn open. They got out of the car, and walked the short distance to the cottage. There were also two guards standing on the small porch, and one leaned over to open the door for them. As Roger entered, he took a quick architectural inventory of the place, noticing a staircase immediately in front of him as he entered. It had a broken banister, and each step was littered and dust-covered.

To the right was a small study that, amidst the clutter and trash, looked as if it had been hastily converted into a meeting area with a new table and four black chairs—the only thing on the walls was some wire, and an occasional nail. Roger noticed that to the left was a larger living area. The clutter had been pushed to one corner to accommodate the several people now working in what had become a makeshift mini-command center. There were two women and a naval seaman sitting at dull-gray desks, all three were on a phone, and would occasionally break away from their conversations to compare notes. Another man, dressed in a British Navy captain's uniform, which Roger recognized as being identical to Clive's, seemed to be overseeing the other three, and at that moment was waiting for the man on the phone to give him some information. A soldier was working on a big wall map of lower England and Northern France. It took Roger only a second to see that the colored pins and string that crisscrossed the map were the paths that Clive would have already followed in green, and that the red strings and pins were the route he was expected to follow on his return. On the same map, there were blue pins and strings, but these seemed to take a different path, and Roger assumed these were the roads and destinations the other team was to follow on their quest for Rotor IV.

As Roger, Alan, and the admiral entered, those in the room briefly looked up from their work, then went about their business.

"Let's go in here," Welles said, gesturing towards the table and chairs that sat in the small study. Roger noticed again that Welles' large sideburns always moved as he spoke, giving him the appearance of a puppet. "Joan," he said to his assistant, " three cups of tea, please."

The three men each took a seat, and Roger tried to absorb everything he had just been told. He was absolutely elated that something had happened that now made Clive a top commodity, and that he needed a whole task force to assure his safe return. At the same time, however, Roger realized that Clive wasn't home yet, and there was still work to be done to get him out of harms way.

"As we were discussing," Welles said, "after the first mission's landing vessel capsized and sank, we were left with the question of what to do. By this time, Clive had already landed, and was well on his way into occupied France, so there was no possibility of contacting him, or recalling him in any way."

The admiral's assistant appeared and slid the cups of tea in front of each of them, Welles looked up and smiled at her, and she smiled back, and it was obvious to both Alan and Roger that there was more to that smile than it appeared.

"So," Admiral Welles continued, "we raced to contact the French Resistance, and immediately opened a line of communication. Once this was done, we informed them of the unfortunate business of the vessel's sinking, and appealed to them for their further assistance in getting the real rotor to Captain Westmore. Once we promised to make up for the sunken supplies and ammunition, they agreed."

"And this," Roger asked, motioning to the commotion around them, "has only just taken place?"

"Only over the past several hours, Mr. Mathews. We are moving with great expediency." He gestured with his large arm towards the other room, from where the sounds of a hushed busyness emanated. "You see, gentlemen, at this moment Captain Westmore is in Arras, and he has probably already determined that the rotor he has been given is a fake."

"So," Alan now spoke, "if Captain Westmore had been set up by you to be caught by the Nazis, why hasn't this happened yet? It would seem that your communications are good enough to determine that he made it safely to Arras."

"I'm glad you brought that up, professor, because I was just getting to that." The admiral leaned towards them, as if what he had to say was of the utmost secrecy. "You see, we are considering ourselves very lucky that we didn't lose Captain Westmore's ship last night as well. It's been determined that a Nazi U-boat had been precisely in the area as the captain's landing vessel neared the shore."

"How do you know this?" asked Roger.

"We picked up a wireless signal from precisely that location from the German submarine U-98, which was returning from touring the Atlantic. Now, the most fascinating thing here is that the message from the U-98's wireless room basically said that it had intercepted a weak message from the British regarding a mission to retrieve secret information about the Enigma machine in Arras."

"But I thought you said that the Germans had already known that Clive was heading to Arras," Roger remarked.

"And so they had, but this message from the German U-98 informed their army post in Boulogne that, according to this newly intercepted message, the venue had changed, and that the Enigma information was to be handed over in Liévin, a full twenty miles away from Arras. Here, take a look for yourself," the admiral said, pushing a piece of paper across for Roger and Alan to look at together.

February 28, 1941

Interception of wireless message from British to suspected French Resistance.

British place of exchange of Enigma information in Arras has changed.

Exchange now to take place in Liévin. Alert all authorities.

Josef Vlauss, Radioman 49j99Lib - U-98

"And how did the German U-boat get this information?" Alan asked, looking up from the paper.

"We haven't the slightest idea," the admiral replied. "We have kept this entire plan in the strictest secrecy, and we can find very few places where a leak could occur. What's more, even if it had been a leak, why would it offer such erroneous information? Never once did I hear the city of Liévin mentioned at any stage of the planning for these missions. So, you see, we have no idea why U-98 would send such a message, but we're most happy that they did."

"So, the German's believed this information was accurate," Alan asked.

"Yes, it would seem so. Our contacts in France indicate that the regiment of Nazi SS troops that went to Arras to search for Captain Westmore was delivered this erroneous message at around one thirty in the morning, and within half an hour they had packed up and were out of Arras, apparently heading for Liévin."

"Admiral," Roger asked, "if you have contacts in the area, why can't they alert Captain Westmore about this new scenario?"

"Because doing so would seriously imperil our contact,

which would then put everyone at risk, and so we work with the knowledge that's given us when we get it. Right now the captain is ignorant of the other mission, and certainly of what is happening now. At least up to that time where the dummy Enigma rotor is placed in his hands."

The three men sat silently for a minute. Roger was mulling over every piece of information he had just heard. He was, of course, ecstatic to hear that Clive was still alive, and that everything possible was now being done to get him back safely. However, he was concerned about how Clive's knowledge of the mission being a decoy would affect what was being done to rescue him. Clive must certainly still presume nothing has changed. Roger was also perplexed about the serendipitous, yet erroneous, message from the German U-boat. How did the Nazis get this information in the first place, he wondered, and how could they be so wrong? Roger noticed the admiral's secretary coming into the room.

"Telephone call, Admiral," she said with a soft Mancunian accent. Roger was becoming surprised at his ability to recognize the many accents that divided England's geography.

"Pardon me, gentlemen," he said, his large frame rising from the chair.

"Admiral, can we step outside to stretch our legs?" Roger asked.

"Of course—we all need a little break, and it looks to be a sunny day out there," the admiral agreed. "You two enjoy it, and let's meet back here in about ten minutes."

"Thank you, sir," Roger said as he and Alan stood up.

They walked to the door, which Alan opened and held for Roger to pass through. They said hello to the two guards, and walked down the overgrown path towards the driveway. A waist-high stucco wall squared the front yard of the cottage, and like the corners of the cottage itself, was overgrown in certain areas with vines and weeds. Roger pulled a pack of cigarettes from his breast pocket and offered one to Alan, who took it and waited for the light.

"So," Roger said, bringing a lit match to Alan's cigarette, and then his own. "What do you think?"

"Well, I think that it's amazing, these turns of events."

"Yeah, me too. But you know, I just don't understand this guy Pomboi. There's just something I don't like about him, I don't know what it is. He's behind this mission with your government, but when things start getting hairy, he leaves. And I don't trust his accent, it's really faint, but it's there."

"Um, Roger, I have something I must tell you."

"Yes, Alan, what is it."

"You cannot repeat this to anyone, ever. I'm trusting you upon everything our friendship rests upon." He motioned for them to go through the gate. They crossed the small driveway, towards the bluff, where their view of the water below was wider, and they could see gulls riding the waves that crashed on the rocks below.

"Okay, what is it, Alan," Roger asked earnestly. "You know you can trust me."

"That's good, because what I'm about to tell you could have me arrested, and maybe worse."

"Alan, my God, what is it?"

"All right then, remember when we were leaving to come to Pevensey, and I ran back into my office to get a piece of the Enigma that I had forgotten. Well, the piece that I ran back to get was nothing more than a small wireless transmitter."

"Okay, but I still don't know where this is headed."

"Oh, you will in a second, old friend," Alan answered back. "To make a long story short…hmmm…how to say this. Well, Roger, simply put, there was no German U-boat."

"What? What do you mean there was no U-boat? They have the message that was sent from U-98. How could they have an actual, transmitted message if there was no…" Roger paused a moment. "Alan, are you about to tell me what I think you're about to tell me?"

"Yes, Roger, I was the submarine U-98."

"But Alan…" Roger was dumbstruck, and looked behind him to make sure no one was around. He leaned closer to Alan. "How did you do it? They think it originated from a specific U-boat, the Germans really fell for it. I can't believe this, why did you do it?"

"Well, Roger, originally it was true. I was going to test a new piece to my Enigma machine, and I did want that to be a secret because I'm not so sure how it would work, and didn't want to announce it to my colleagues quite yet. When you came to me yesterday, and told me all about the mission being a decoy, and that our governments were sending our man Clive into a trap, I was really tested by it. So, I finally figured that if the Germans were directed away from Arras, and therefore Clive, it would heighten his chances for getting out once he determined the rotor he was given was not real." A gull cried out over the water, and Alan took a last drag off his cigarette, dropping the butt on the ground and stepping on it.

"I also didn't want to jeopardize the other team," Alan continued, "because after all, they were to get the actual rotor, which is something we really need in order to start breaking the German Navy's Enigma codes. So, I determined that directing the Nazis to Liévin would give the Captain a chance to escape, while at the same time making sure that the other team was not jeopardized."

"I cannot believe what I'm hearing," Roger said, shaking his head with a half-grin. "But how did you send the signal, how did you encode it, how did you make it look like it came from a specific U-boat?"

"U-boat U-98, you mean. Well, I knew when we were still in Bletchley Park that I needed to do this, and so while I was in my hut getting the transmitter, I quickly referred to a book we have that lists all of the transmissions of coded messages we intercept from the Germans. It lists the time it was sent and the naval ship or army corps that was sending it. In some cases, we even know the name of the German radioman who encrypted and radioed the message. Well, using this, I was able to determine that U-98 was due back into port around the twenty-ninth of this month. So, I basically made them arrive a bit ahead of schedule, and made it such that as they were passing the British Coast, they intercepted this message, falsely directing them to Liévin. Knowing that U-98 was not yet in the area, I could safely send the message without it being picked up by the wireless transmitter on board. Had they intercepted the message, they would have immediately alerted the ground forces that they had received a message from an imposter."

Roger stood, staring and blinking, amazed by it all.

"Okay, so how did you know that the Germans on shore wouldn't know that U-98 wasn't due back in port for another two days?"

"I didn't. To everything, Roger, there is an element of chance, and this was that element. With that in mind, and seeing that most U-boats were usually a few days ahead or behind schedule, I was pretty sure that the German forces on the coast, who are usually not as strict about things as the German Navy, would probably not look up on their charts to see when U-98 should be returning."

"And so apparently, they bought it," Roger offered with a smile.

"Apparently they did. As did His Majesty's Navy."

"Alan," Roger said gently. "Why did you do it?"

"Because you were so distraught, Roger, and because I'm your friend. You know, I still have feelings for you, and because of that, I'd go out of my way. But also, I had a moral dilemma to deal with, because I wasn't sure if I could take part in a plan than was putting a man directly in harm's way, for the very purpose of being harmed. Add to that the fact that I've come to like Captain Westmore—well, it was the least I could do."

"Alan, I can't believe you did this. What's more, I can't believe you pulled it off."

"Well, pulling it off is still a question that needs to be determined." He looked over his shoulder towards the ramshackle cottage. "The fact that Clive doesn't know this change in plans yet, and that he is probably still believing his to be a decoy mission, makes it somewhat dangerous. Do you think we should come clean, so to speak, and tell the admiral everything."

Roger thought for a moment, and took a breath as he looked out towards the gray sea, its waves white capped with froth and foam. All he wanted at this point was Clive back safe and sound. Alan raised a good question, he thought to himself, and for a second he put himself in Clive's place. Knowing that Clive had intended to go ahead with the decoy mission despite its inevitable trap, he made up his mind pretty quickly.

"No, we say nothing," Roger answered finally. "Firstly, we have to remember that like a dumb fool, Clive said that he was going to go ahead with the mission as if there were no decoy, no second team, no change in plans. My God, now I'm glad that he's so stubborn and dutiful. Secondly, it's obvious that this information wouldn't affect the new plans to have the French Resistance intercept Clive and give him the real rotor, and lastly, I'm not having you get into trouble. So, we say nothing."

"All right, then," Alan concurred. "I was half-thinking the same thing anyway, but wanted to put it on the table for discussion. Then, we're agreed. Shall we go back in?" he asked smiling, and the two men started towards the cottage. They took two steps when Roger stopped in mid-step.

"Alan, I can't say enough to thank you for what you did. I mean, Clive coming back was something I really didn't think was going to happen, and now, largely because of you, he will."

"You can show me your gratitude some other time," Alan said, smiling and winking his eye provocatively. Roger laughed and put his arm around Alan's shoulder as they crossed the road, and walked up the path to the steps of the cottage. The early morning sun cast a rosy light on the front of the small building, and warmed their faces. They turned to look out on the water once again before going in. It was going to be a long day, and probably an even longer night. The guard was already holding the door open for them, so they turned and went into the busy cottage. Their mission now was to bring Clive home.

CHAPTER V: EVASION

The old man turned away from the sea and looked inland. From this higher up spot, he could see over the many fields and hews of trees, and if he squinted just right, far in the distance the house they had shared. He recalled the parties and their friends, and the old man thought about their many holidays to Greece. They had travelled well through life; that was until the other day.

The bodies of the two Nazi guards were still in the truck when they pulled into downtown Arras. Claudette, who was driving at this point, seemed to know the streets of Arras well, and Clive assumed she must have spent quite a bit of time there. Suddenly, Claudette steered down an alley between the walls of an abandoned factory, and then drove the truck through a large door that led into the factory's cavernous mechanics shop, where they parked and waited. They didn't have to wait long before the group of French Resistance Fighters appeared, and took positions around their truck.

"Hello, Spider," Claudette said to the bearded face that appeared in the window next to Clive. "I'd like you to meet Captain Clive Westmore."

"A pleasure," said the man, maneuvering his hand through the opened window and shaking Clive's. He was middle-aged, dressed almost entirely in black, and his salt and pepper hair was combed straight back. He was obviously their leader, Clive thought, and was most likely the one person who was in possession of the rotor. Spider opened the door for Clive, who slid off the seat, thankful he no longer had to ride in a truck.

"We had a slight problem a little while ago," Claudette said, opening her door and walking around the front of the truck to where Clive and Spider stood.

"And what might that have been?" Spider asked, but by this time Claudette had already started walking to the back of the truck. Spider and Clive had just caught up with her as she was loosening the straps holding the back doors closed. She opened the doors, and as she did, one of the soldier's hands dropped out, its fingers pointing accusingly at Claudette.

"Ah, I see," Spider said, reaching over and flipping the arm back across the soldier's lifeless body. "So, how did this happen?"

"We had arranged for Chloe to keep one of the guards at the checkpoint occupied, but instead, both were there, and they seemed very suspicious," Claudette answered. "While searching the inside of the truck, they discovered the faux bread and wire mesh that was hiding the guns and ammunition. They pulled their guns, and having no other choice, Clive had to shoot them."

"Did you leave any evidence?" Spider asked.

"No, I doused the place in perfume, and strategically left a lipstick lying where it might be found. As there was no blood, it will be assumed that the men were having an encounter with their girls. However, by mid-day today, I'm sure the investigators will be called in."

"We'll take them from here," Spider said, snapping his finger, causing two resistance fighters who were standing near to move into action. They hoisted the bodies over their shoulders, and disappeared through a door that seemed to lead into blackness.

"Your cover was a good idea," Spider said, "but it's unfortunate that you had to kill checkpoint guards in the first place. You see, because the enemy sympathetically views them as sitting ducks at the hands of the Resistance, their deaths have elicited an angry response from the Nazis in the past. It compels them to exact revenge by rounding up suspected Resistance members and shooting them in front of their children. Worse, they're usually wrong in who they suspect, and so innocent people die. Nevertheless, we'll move the bodies to a vacant apartment we know, and make it look like they were killed by their whores. What kind of gun did you use?" Spider asked Clive.

"A French made M76." Clive's voice echoed off the walls of the dark and empty factory.

"Excellent, you cover yourself well, captain. I was afraid if it were an English gun, the bullets would easily have clued the Germans that they came from an Englishman. How lucky for us you enjoy killing with our guns."

"Monsieur Spider," Clive declared, not liking what the Frenchman was implying, "I do not like killing at all."

"Not even brutal Nazis?" Spider asked.

"No, not even brutal Nazis."

"Spider," Claudette asked, stepping between the two, "what do you know about the soldiers that came into town late last night and then left quickly, what was that?"

"We don't know," Spider said, running his hands through his hair. "It doesn't happen very often, and if I didn't know better myself, I would have thought they were on to our Englishman here."

"But how would they know? she asked. "And why would they come, then leave after a few hours?" "Again, we have no idea," Spider answered shrugging. "They're gone—good riddance, good night."

"Monsieur Spider," Clive said with a remindful cough, "there's still a little business needing to be taken care of."

"Oh, yes, of course," Spider said, snapping his fingers again. Immediately one of the men who had been standing watch at a window walked over with a small leather bag and handed it to Spider. He undid the small latch, withdrew the rotor, and gave it to Clive.

"Here is your Holy Grail, here is what you came for," he said as Clive started examining it immediately. Within seconds he had determined that, as had been foretold by Roger, this was indeed a fake rotor. He had never doubted that it would be fake, however he was wishing with one last grain of hope that the rotor would be real.

"Thank you," Clive said to Spider, who took the rotor back, put it in the small leather bag, then handed the bag back to

Clive.

"We have been here too long, and we have these guards to take care of, so we must be going," throwing his coat on with a flourish. He kissed Claudette on each cheek, then shook Clive's hand.

"Monsieur Captain, good luck. You may need it."

"Thank you, Monsieur Spider," Clive responded, with little warmth.

Spider climbed into the truck's passenger seat. One of his men had already started the truck, and was waiting for him.

"Would you like an escort back to your apartment?" Spider asked, leaning out the window. "The rest of my men will be back soon."

"Thank you, but I think we'd rather not wait, but get home as soon as possible," Claudette replied. With that the truck made a three-point turn in the large chamber, and disappeared through the same opening that Claudette had driven through earlier. They stood and listened to the grinding of the truck's gears and the rumbling of its engines until it disappeared, leaving them in cold silence.

It was a short but exhausting walk to Claudette's apartment, and the sky was light with the morning sun. It was a cold morning, with gray clouds hanging low like a ceiling.

Clive was in Claudette's apartment now, sipping Turkish coffee and sitting on a fitted bench nestled up against the large bay window that looked five stories down upon the Rue de Cambrai. Claudette's was one of those old French apartment buildings that had been built during the Napoleonic era, or maybe even earlier. It reminded him of Roger's apartment, and he wondered what Roger was doing that moment. Claudette had gone to the market for food, and Clive was left to his own devices. He got up from the bench, and walked into the large open living space and to the bay broad window.

He looked out, admiring the small city, and thought about how totally unprepared France had been to battle the invading Nazis. Most French cities fell easily to the Germans, and so there was little in Arras that would indicate the Warmacht had passed through it. The only evidence that something was not right was the Nazi soldiers who occasionally patrolled the streets, and even now, his eyes followed two of them as they walked down the street. Yes, he was in German occupied France again, and although it usually filled him with great excitement in the past, he was beginning to have second thoughts about it this time—he wanted to be home with Roger. Nevertheless, there was a duty to be done, a debt to his mother's country that needed to be repaid. He hated the Nazis for the vile defiling of his mother's country, and the violation of its people. He walked into the kitchen, poured another coffee, and went back to looking out the window.

He recalled his first mission, not too long after the Nazis invaded France, where he witnessed firsthand the thousands being rounded up. His contacts in France were beginning to receive rumored reports about what was happening to these people—that they were being rounded up and shipped east, to Czechoslovakia and Poland, to what at the time were being called holding camps. Movement on the street below caught Clive's eye, as a Nazi army truck, filled with a contingent of soldiers, drove by.

He looked at his feet, where sat a small leather bag that contained the fake rotor. He reached in and pulled the imposter out. With its grooves and slots, he saw how it could be confused for the real thing, but when he held it up to Alan's list of what made an authentic rotor, it sadly, though expectedly, failed. He watched another pair of Nazi soldiers walk down the street, or maybe it was the same two he saw earlier. Their rifles, like long primal spears, hung from their shoulders, and he was reminded of the two checkpoint guards he had killed. He had been forced to kill only once before, and hated to think there could ever be a time he could get used to it.

He heard keys rattling outside the door, and followed them as they made their way to the keyhole and unlocked the door. The door swung open, and Claudette entered carrying two sacks.

"It's gotten colder," she remarked, removing the scarf that enveloped her head.

"I hope we don't get snow. That would not be good right now."

"I don't think so. I can usually smell snow, and I'm not smelling it now."

"I hope you're right," Clive said, picking up the two sacks and following Claudette into the kitchen.

"You must be hungry," Claudette said. "Give me a few minutes and I'll make us something."

Clive went into the living area, grabbed a magazine from the coffee table, and laid down on the sofa to read. Within minutes, the smell of sausages and frying potatoes filled the apartment. The scent brought him back to more comfortable times, and he felt relaxed, despite being in the middle of a jaded mission. They would while away the hours until tonight, when they would leave Arras, and head back to Boulogne. He was still not sure what to make of the regiment of Nazi soldiers that came and quickly left the night before. What could it have meant? Could they have been looking for someone else? Could it have been a new policy the Nazis were initiating to flush out the Resistance? Worse, could they have discovered the plans of the other team, and were racing to capture them? He didn't know, nor could he guess, and so his intentions were to simply follow his initial plan. With that thought, he resumed reading the magazine, and waited for Claudette to serve up breakfast.

The apartment door jiggled, and then suddenly swung open. Clive quickly and instinctively reached for his pistol, which had been sitting on the coffee table next to him. The middle-aged woman who entered was thin and pretty, but with a strong, stoical face framed by dark blond hair that poked through the red kerchief she wore on her head. Clive, still reclining on the sofa, pistol in hand, watched as she sat the large cloth bag she was carrying in a corner near the door. She looked over at him for a moment, saw the gun in his hand, rolled her eyes and shook her head disapprovingly, as if he were a child with a toy gun. She neither smiled nor gave any acknowledgement to Clive, other than to keep her eyes on him as she removed her gloves and shoved them in her coat. She cocked her head towards the kitchen.

"I'm home," the woman said, removing her coat. At this point, although confused, Clive placed the gun back on the table.

"Good," came Claudette's reply from the kitchen. "You are in time for breakfast."

The woman walked over to the large table that served as desk and dinette, picked up an envelope from a pile of papers, and casually looked at it, flipping it over and back, not necessarily reading, but more preparing to say something.

"So, Monsieur," she finally said, "you have made it here at last, eh?" She didn't look up as she spoke, but continued admiring the envelope.

"Yes, I am Captain Westmore," Clive said, rising from the sofa and walking towards her with an outstretched hand. She looked at it strangely for a second, as if she was not used to people wanting to shake her hand, but slowly placed the envelope back on the table and took Clive's hand in a firm grip.

"It is a pleasure," she said, looking into his eyes only for a second before they darted elsewhere. There was an uncomfortably long moment, as the two just stood there, and Clive was beginning to wish that Claudette would hurry up and get out of the kitchen.

"I am Madeleine," she suddenly blurted.

"Well, Madeleine, once more, it is a pleasure to meet you." He didn't know what to make of this woman, nor did he know how she fit into the picture. She seemed rather young to be Claudette's mother, although she was certainly somewhat older. Maybe a sister, however, the two women shared little facial similarities or coloring. Nevertheless, she was important enough to know who he was, and probably why he was there.

Finally, Claudette entered the room balancing three large serving bowls. Madeleine walked over and took one, and in the same motion leaned over and kissed Claudette gently on the cheek. Claudette smiled at Madeleine.

"It's good to be home," Claudette said. "It was a rather adventurous evening. Please, everybody, sit."

"I still don't like this business with the Resistance," Madeleine responded, pulling out a chair and pushing away some papers that littered the spot where she sat. "It will someday get you into trouble, Claudette."

"Ah, but my France needs me," Claudette said, smiling up towards the ceiling. "More coffee captain?"

"Yes, please." Clive pushed his cup towards her.

Breakfast was spent discussing that night's plans for making it back to Boulogne. Claudette had things arranged perfectly, and they would leave shortly after eleven, driving in a car she had arranged, and posing as newlyweds on their way back home to the coast from their wedding. They expected to be on the beach waiting for the rendezvous party shortly after two-thirty in the morning. They wanted to leave themselves enough time, because the rendezvous party would not wait around, and had implicit instructions to leave and return to England if Clive didn't show up by three-thirty in the morning. Throughout the conversation, which was basically just between Clive and Claudette, Madeleine watched them intently, as if she were trying to understand how and why they got along so well. The few questions she had asked Clive led him to believe she was somewhat jealous. Of course, having gone through what they had the night before, he and Claudette were naturally closer than most first acquaintances, but Madeleine seemed to be looking intently for something more.

The meal finished, Claudette and Madeleine got up and began collecting the plates and bowls. Clive watched them go into the kitchen towards the rear of the flat, and his position afforded him the ability to see through the large doorway and into a part of the kitchen. He was thinking about Roger, and how much he missed him, and wanted to get back and hold him. But his eyes caught something that made him lose this thought, because through his line of sight into the kitchen, he could see Claudette and Madeleine kissing. It was not a kiss of friendship, either, but was romantic, passionate, and amorous. He watched as their hands moved over each other in ways that were not lacking in familiarity. Clive now grasped why Madeleine seemed somewhat jealous, and why these two women lived in the apartment together. He had never really given much thought to lesbians, and had never actually known one, either. He knew little of them, but knew he shared a common bond, and therefore should understand their situation and the societal pressures that drove lesbians and homosexuals underground. Driving them into worlds that at times were dark and shadowy, but nonetheless filled with sparks of light, like warm dark summer nights filled with fireflies that blinked and glittered.

He watched as they pulled from their kiss, and Madeleine whispered something to Claudette, who laughed and whispered her response. The two came closer one more time, as if they were dancing, and then parted, the moment gone. Claudette's eyes fell on Clive, and realized he had seen, she looked at him for a second, and then smiled. He smiled back, but also nodded, to show that he understood. Still smiling, she disappeared out of view, and Clive continued to hear the two women chatting in the kitchen as he got up from the table, walked to the window seat, and picked up the bag that sat on the floor. He once again pulled out the rotor, and looked at it. Who could think that this round disc, the size of a small salad plate, could drag him into deepest occupied France? He ran his fingers along the serrated ridge, which was one of the indications that this rotor was an imposter. He looked out the window, and thought about Roger, and how he was probably one of the more handsome men with whom Clive had ever entered into a relationship. He had experienced a number of encounters with men who were wonderfully attractive and sexual, but Roger had many personal qualities that rounded things tremendously; his intelligence for one thing, and his quickness to laugh and poke fun. At times he was so American, too, using funny Americanisms that sometimes Clive could only understand in their context. He wished Roger was with him now, and thought about kissing him, and holding him. The last time they were together like that had been only a few days ago, but it already felt like weeks.

They had just got back from dinner, where they had finished up the final bit of work while eating at their favorite pub; another twelve-hour day. Throughout dinner they sat as close as two gentlemen could when going over papers at a table. Clive would occasionally, caress Roger's leg with his foot under the table. He knew this annoyed Roger, who never liked taking chances in public, but Clive continued, knowing the tablecloth hid everything, and because he knew that although it bothered Roger, he liked the attention and touch.

Their cab ride home was nicer, with their work for the day finally finished, they held hands in the darkness of the back of the cab, and even then only under Clive's coat that sat between them on the seat. Clive liked holding hands, and would gently stroke Roger's, exploring his long fingers, the cup of his palm, his wrist and lower arm. He loved Roger's hands, and someday he was going to set about getting out his oils and rendering them on canvas. When they got back to Roger's they were both excited, and couldn't wait to take each other in their arms. Leaving their cases and coats by the door as they entered, they headed straight for the sofa, where they talked and kissed. They sat there for a while, exploring each other's bodies, and although the exploration seemed somewhat redundant—these were, by now, well-charted waters—the excitement never seemed to abate. Clive brought his hands up, slowly opened Roger's shirtfront, and started kissing Roger's stomach and chest. Clive worked his lips to Roger's nipples, and then to his neck, and finally to Roger's lips, where they played and danced. Clive reached over and powerfully, though gently, pulled Roger up by the lapel, and removed the rest of Roger's shirt, his lean body gently resting back onto the sofa.

"Are you all right?" he asked tenderly, wanting to make sure Roger was as comfortable as possible. Tonight, Clive wanted to give, tend to, and serve.

"I'm fine," Roger replied quietly, waited a second then added, "I love you."

"I love you, too," Clive gently replied. He leaned in and kissed Roger once again, their tongues dancing an erotic waltz. He reached down and undid Roger's belt, and stood him up so that he could slide off Roger's pants and underwear. This done, he removed his own shirt, and opened his trousers, then gently moved the now naked Roger back to the couch. He made sure Roger was comfortable, lying on the couch, and over the next twenty minutes, proceeded to perform several unbridled acts that left Roger spent, and panting in total ecstasy. Clive laid his head on Roger's heaving stomach, and the two remained in this position for a while, after which they proceeded to the bedroom, the night still young. Roger reciprocated Clive's performance with his own, and the two men spent most of the night lost in a passionate, no-holds-barred, take-no-prisoner escapade of pleasure and play.

"More coffee, Monsieur," a voice interrupted. It was Madeleine.

"Oh, no thank you, I'm about to turn in, I think," Clive said, crossing his legs to hide the enormous erection he had. Madeleine returned to the kitchen, and Clive stood up and walked the four steps to the window. Despite the coffee he had for breakfast, he was exhausted, and made his way to the sofa, where he stretched out, putting his stocking feet up on an arm rest, a small square pillow supporting his head. He thought of Roger again, and how he wanted him, and yes, even needed him. He had to get back, and he would stop at nothing to do so. If all of Hitler's armies stood in his way, he'd plow through them to return to Roger. But that was a battle he would have to handle later that night. His move from consciousness to sleep was seamless.

He woke up only twice. The first around two-thirty in the afternoon by the telephone ringing. It seemed to ring for a very long time, and Clive was almost ready to either answer it, or yank the wire from the wall. He noticed that he had been draped with a blanket, the apartment left empty. The second time was around four, and the women were still out. He used the water closet, and was back asleep within a minute of returning to the couch. He dreamt of sinking ships, men screaming as their mouths filled with briny water, and then the faint cry of women. Then there were no more dreams, just sleep.

"Monsieur Captain," Claudette's voice roused him. "It is time to eat."

"What time is it?" Clive asked, rubbing his eyes.

"It is almost eight o'clock, and we'll need to eat and finish preparing to leave," came the gentle reply. Clive looked out the window and it was already night—although it was just after dusk, there were still pink wisps of clouds back-dropped by navy blue skies.

"I'll be ready." He sat up and yawned. He hated sleeping during the day and getting up to work at night, it was very disorienting. But he did what he had to, and his excellent physical condition made it easier for him to return to a normal sleeping pattern afterwards. Claudette disappeared into the kitchen, from where the sounds of dinner preparation were emanating.

He was about to leave Arras having not been captured by the Germans, and this threw him—he didn't know why they hadn't come for him. Could they have decided it wasn't worth it? He didn't think so, if the Nazis believed an enigma rotor was going to fall into a British agent's hands, they certainly wouldn't sit on it. He was certain the regiment of Nazi soldiers was sent to Arras to find him and the rotor. But, if they knew his itinerary, which was sent to them courtesy of His Majesty's government, then certainly they would have known of his intentions of hiding in Arras during the day, and not leaving before nightfall. So, why did they leave so early after entering the city? What made them turn around? He just couldn't fathom it. He did know one thing, though, and that was that Roger was probably missing him, and fearing the worst had already befallen him. He got up from the sofa, and began to get ready. It was going to be one hell of a night.

Alan slid another cup of tea in front of Roger, who nodded gratefully. They were in the busy map room as it was now being called, and Roger was just getting off the phone with Jean Pierre in London.

"Well, he has not heard from his people in several hours," Roger said, looking over at Admiral Welles.

"I'm sure there's a good explanation." Welles replied. "Remember, our sources there are good, and have informed us they made it to Arras safely." The admiral was sitting a few feet away on another telephone, waiting for someone at the other end to find a specific document to read to him over the phone. Roger had noticed that when Welles was on the phone, his accent became very affected and formal, and sounding like that dying breed of Englishman who were the remnants of an old England, and a British Empire upon which the sun never set.

"We'll continue working on the assumption that they're still there," the Admiral said. "Again, we know from our sources that they're in Arras, so as long as the Nazi regiment has left, leaving just the regular forces, Clive is safe for the time being… Ah, yes, that's the one…please read that to me…" The admiral started talking into the phone.

"I'm sure he's right," Alan said, sliding down into the chair next to Roger. "It sounds to me as if this Claudette is everything her brother says she is. Oh, how did this Pierre react when you told him that he, too, had been deceived by his own people? I saw your face and I inferred he wasn't too happy."

"He was nonchalant about it, which somewhat surprised me," Roger said, swiveling in his chair to face Alan.

"You don't think he somehow knew about the deception, too, now do you?" Alan asked incredulously.

"I don't know. It's possible he's just very businesslike, and that his being deceived by his superiors in the French Resistance is par for the course." Roger's voice lowered a bit, so that only Alan could hear. "I just wish I knew what Clive was doing right now. Is he safe, is he being taken care of by the guide, what?"

"Roger, my friend, I'm sure the captain's doing his best to get home to you."

Clive was drinking tea at the table in the dining area. After dinner, they still had a few hours before they needed to leave. Claudette and Madeleine relaxed on the sofa, while Clive readied himself for the trip. He sat at the dining table for a while, cleaning his pistol, which gave him something to concentrate on. While he was cleaning, he thought about Madeleine, wondering why she seemed so irritated throughout dinner, and how at one point had even asked why one of the other Resistance members couldn't take Clive back to Boulogne. However, Claudette had just smiled and said it was her job, and that having gotten to know Clive so much more, she wouldn't leave it to anyone else.

Clive had finished cleaning his pistol, and was now sitting on a chair near a lamp, reviewing the paperwork that Claudette had falsified. They were to be Mr. and Mrs. Stephan Tanabre, just married, and on their way home to Boulogne. Claudette had borrowed a large car, and it was already filled with small pieces of furniture, clocks, boxes, and other home-like articles that would give the sense that they had been given a lot of wedding gifts and things for their new home.

"But upon which wall to hang our lovely new rotor," he said under his breath, half-jokingly.

"Did you say something?" Madeleine asked from the kitchen.

"No, I was just talking to myself."

The hour had finally come, and they were up and about, getting ready to leave, and Claudette and Madeleine moved into the kitchen to say good-bye to one another. Again, from where he stood, he could see their tender farewell, and wished that his and Roger's had been similar. He wondered about the differences between being a lesbian and being a homosexual. He would like to ask Claudette, and even discuss his own homosexuality with her, but it was impossible. He had been conditioned to stay silent even if he was pretty certain he was safe with the person he was talking to. He had taken a great chance with Roger, because he had not completely determined that Roger was homosexual, but worse, had risked an advance on someone he was involved with professionally, and on a top-secret mission at that. However, the signals that he'd picked up from Roger were not overly cryptic, nor did they need an Enigma machine to be understood. It had felt right, and so he'd moved on his assumption. Now, seeing the passionate and tender kisses the two women were sharing, he wished he had Roger with him now.

Clive would drive. They got into the car that Claudette had earlier moved to the front of the apartment building, they looked up to see Madeleine silhouetted in the large window. She waved once, then disappeared from view. It was a cold and dry night, but there was a smell of newly thawed soil in the air that suggested Spring might be around the corner. They would leave Arras using a different route from the one they entered, thinking that if the Nazi's had discovered the two dead soldiers, the guardhouse from where they supposedly disappeared would be overrun by the SS. They drove out on the Rue de Cambrai, and soon came to the Cambrai guardhouse.

"Ready, Madam Tanabre?" Clive asked, as they approached.

"Yes, dear husband," Claudette joked back. Clive slowed the car, and came to a halt at the small barricade that blocked their path. A soldier came out of the guardhouse and walked up to the driver's window, which Clive had already rolled down.

"Papers," was all the young man said. As Clive handed them their false identification, he noticed the guard was quite handsome.

"And where are you going tonight Monsieur?" the guard asked in rather bad French.

"We are going to our new home," Claudette interjected.

"We just got married, and are joining my husband's family in Boulogne."

The guard nodded.

"Congratulations," he said, and then putting his fingers to his lips whistled. From the guardhouse came a rather rotund, middle-aged soldier.

"Just a couple of married Frenchies," he said in German, Clive understanding at least some of what the handsome soldier said. Clive could read and understand some German, but could barely speak it. "But I think we should poke around the trunk a bit," the young soldier added.

"They're going to search the car, I think," Clive whispered to Claudette. They looked at each other with slight shrugs, and Clive followed her gaze to the back of the car, where in a box of books, was a hollowed out tome, and whose cavity held the fake rotor. He had asked himself shortly after receiving the faux piece if it was worth his carrying around and pretending it was the real McCoy, but he decided that he should follow his mission to the letter, as he said he would, and maybe if he got back to England, the fake piece might shed light on something. Clive noticed that Claudette was crossing her fingers.

The larger Nazi waddled to the car, opened the back door and started rifling through the boxes, bags, and furniture stuffed in the back. The younger one did the same on the other side. A box shifted and dislodged from its position.

"Be careful with our belongings," Claudette demanded. "Some of that is fragile."

"We'll be mindful," the younger Nazi said. "Be careful you clod," he said in German to the older soldier.

After a few minutes, it was obvious the two were not looking for anything special, but were merely tossing things here and there. Clive was relieved about this, because on top of the fact that these two guards seemed somewhat inexperienced, it meant that the bodies of the two soldiers he killed had probably yet to be found. Nevertheless, by now they were obviously known to be missing, and that was bad enough.

"See anything suspicious, Gerthardt?" the young man asked.

"No," was the only word the large man said, closing the car's door.

"Here are your papers," the young Nazi said, handing them through the window. "You're free to go."

"Thank you," Clive said, taking the scrolled-up documents, which the soldier held onto a bit longer than he should, forcing Clive's eyes up and into the handsome face of the soldier.

"Have a good evening," the young man said, smiling in a way Clive well recognized.

"Yes, you, too." Clive smiled back at the handsome guard. He held the soldier's gaze for a moment, waved, then drove onward into the night.

Wanting to avoid as many major roads as possible, their path would take them on the E15 from Arras, then tthe N42 as originally planned by Clive and Roger, all the way up to the area of Boulogne. It would be a long drive. Neither of them could guess how many times they might be stopped and searched, and so it was important that they gave themselves as much time as possible.

Roger and Alan had returned to the inn at Pevensey around four in the afternoon to clean up and rest, mostly at the Admiral's urging, and although it was nice to be clean and in fresh clothes, Roger couldn't sleep. Alan, however, fell quickly into slumber and was snoring in the large bed that took up most of the room. Roger sat at a small table, going over a map of Northern France. He looked up, rubbed his eyes, and wished he could sleep. He wasn't going to have the chance again until after Clive got back. It felt strange, because yesterday at this time he was sure Clive was not going to return at all, and now, God willing, sometime in the wee hours of tomorrow morning, he would return—that is if the French Resistance met up with him before the Nazis.

Before he and Alan left the makeshift command center, an intercepted message from the German Army came in, and a few of the more salient words could be deciphered immediately: "Englishman left Arras" and "heading for coast." The Germans had realized their mistake, that Clive had been in Arras all along, and was now heading back to the coast of France. However, there were other parts to the cryptic message, and more information could have been gleaned if the entire communiqué had been deciphered immediately, but it couldn't. It was now a race between the French and Germans on who would get to Clive first.

Roger quietly slipped out of the room, went down to the proprietor and ordered some dinner that would be brought up to the room. With a small rapping at the door it came about twenty minutes later. He set it out on the small table, then woke Alan.

"Alan, Alan, dinner is here. Come on, wake up."

"Hmmmmm," Alan moaned as he rolled over, propping himself on one elbow and looking around blankly. "What time is it?"

"It's six o'clock, and we should be getting back to the cottage. There's been no call, so I'm assuming there haven't been any new developments. Come on, let's eat so we can get back."

The two men ate quickly and quietly. Roger, who usually didn't like bangers and mash, ordered it because it was the only thing the innkeeper could whip up on such short notice. Nevertheless, he took one bite and realized that he was ravenous, and suddenly couldn't get enough of the stuff, nor could he remember when his last full meal had been. When they finished, they grabbed their coats and drove back to the cottage. It was dusk when they arrived, and everything on the ground was black and colorless, but the sky was still somewhat bright, and small groups of birds would occasionally pepper the sky. They drove up to the two handsome guards at the bottom of the driveway, and once recognized, were waved on.

"I think that blond one likes me," Alan said, turning around to look back as they drove up towards the cottage.

"Yeah, he and Churchill are both dying to have tea with you," Roger said smiling. It was his first real smile in two days.

"No, Roger, I'm serious. I think he winked at me."

"Yeah, well, maybe it's the military's high-sign or something, and it really just means 'have a good day.'" Roger's smile broadened as he pulled the car to a halt behind several others parked in front of the cottage.

"We had a high-sign when I was visiting in America at Princeton four years ago," Alan cheerfully said. "It went something like this," and Alan proceeded to do a strange wave with both hands that looked like he was making outrageous shadow puppets. Roger laughed, and Alan joined in.

"All right, then," Alan conceded. "At least everyone was using it at the time, and so no one was singled out as looking like a complete idiot." They both laughed again. It was good to laugh, and Roger felt all the better for it.

"Let's go in," Roger said resolutely. "We have work to do, my friend."

Someone had lit a fire in the cottage's stone fireplace, and they were greeted with the warm smoky air of the busy command center. It gave a cozy feeling, despite the drab modern-looking office furniture that was spread about the room. The admiral, sitting at the bank of phones, saw them come in, and motioned for them to come over.

"I was just trying to call you in your room," the admiral began. "Our sources have confirmed the German communiqué.

Captain Westmore and his guide have left Arras, and are on their way to Boulogne."

"And what about the French Resistance team that is trying to intercept them with the authentic rotor?" Roger asked.

"They are moving into action, and hopefully can meet up with the captain somewhere in here," the admiral replied, making a small circle on the map with a fat finger. "As is usually the case when events move faster than communications. We have learned that the French Resistance was able to get word to its group with the actual rotor, but were unable to contact their people in the Arras area to get word to the captain."

"But I thought you said you have a contact there, otherwise you wouldn't have gotten this information."

"True, but as I said, our contact there is such a high-level operative that we cannot endanger his presence at this point," the admiral countered. One of the aides walked up and handed him a paper. He looked at it, nodded, and handed it back.

"In any case, at least they're on their way," Alan said.

"Mr. Matthews," the admiral said. "You are sure he'll take the planned route back, aren't you?"

"He's pretty much stuck to the game plan so far, so I see no reason why he'd change now."

"Good. Now let's just hope the French Resistance can catch up with him." The three men turned to look up at the large map with its pins and colored string.

They drove on into the night, occasionally passing a fleet of Nazi trucks and tanks, which left their mark by tearing up the roads, and making them impassable even by French standards. Another eerie thing that Clive noticed was that there seemed to be an ever-increasing number of swastikas that draped the little town halls and other buildings of the villages they passed through. Even in the night, the spidery design would catch his eye, bringing his mind to dark places. Clive thought about his father, who backed Germany right up to its invasion of Poland, and until then thought that Hitler was the best thing that could have happened. That finally, the Germans had a leader who could bring some glory to the country. However, Hitler's appetite was more ravenous than Clive's father had believed, consuming first Germany, then areas of Hungary and Czechoslovakia. As if that wasn't enough, he turned his gluttonous gaze on Poland, always a favorite at banquets of conquest. And it wouldn't have stopped there, had England not declared war. But, his father found out— as did the rest of the world—by then it was too late.

Now England, small, isolated England, was all that stood between Hitler and his mastery over all of Europe. The English on their little island, with the help of the New World, as Churchill called the United States, were standing fast, and doing whatever they could to endure the onslaught. Now, a small part of that defiant England was hurrying past swastikas in a ramshackle old car, with an unusable rotor stowed away in his bag.

"Not a real rotor, mind you," Clive thought to himself, "but a bloody fake one." He smiled sarcastically, and drove on.

His parents had left Blythdale for their annual winter holiday to somewhere that was warm and sunny. The servants still scurried around the place, mending and primping. The number of servants had decreased over the years, and now stood at only four maids and the head butler. He knew their names, and especially liked James, the butler, a somewhat older fellow who on a number of occasions had gone out of his way to make sure that Clive and whoever he brought home were made comfortable. Clive thought James was a homosexual, too, one of those wonderfully gentle souls that was forced to live quiet little lives as servants, clergy, or officers in the military; anything to get away from having to confront who and what they were. So, they chose regimented lives that gave them neither the time nor the opportunity to fulfill their primal desires. In his family's butler, Clive had an accomplice, to whom he was always kind and thoughtful, and would always give nights, and sometimes entire days off when his parents were away from Blythdale.

The fireplace was putting out wonderful heat, when he and Charlie came in from their cold, wet walk through the garden. One thing Clive liked to do when his parents were away was to leave the confines of his little bachelor's suite in the north wing, and take over the whole house. He would lounge in the library reading and studying, or sit at the sixty-foot table in the dining hall and eat his dinner. Tonight, he and Charlie would do just this, and after the servants retired, they might even go to the small music hall, with all of its glitter and mirrors, and dance with each other.

Charlie was the third son of a lesser duke, so his future was certainly wrapped in the collection of aristocratic poor, with barely a title, and worse, forced to get a job. Although Clive was working towards his degree, and had all intentions of working up the pedagogical steps of academia, there was enough of an estate even after his brother became Lord Westmore to keep Clive from having to work. Nevertheless, Clive liked getting his hands dirty, so to speak, and loved the idea of teaching, writing, and researching. He fell quickly for Charlie, who was a student at Oxford as well. Charlie was beautiful, with Nordic features that could only have been a throwback to the invasions of the Vikings. He had a strong square jaw, ocean blue eyes, and hair as blond as white gold. But more, he was smart, fun to be with, and knew a lot, so when they weren't making love, they were in the library trying to prove the other wrong in some debate they were having. Sometimes they would skip lunch because they were engrossed in a conversation about a certain work of Yeats, or some other prolific writer.

"Oh, that fire feels delightful," Charlie said as he moved closer, bending slightly and extending his hands and arms to the warmth. "I think I'll stand like this for the rest of the night."

"Oh, no you won't," Clive retorted laughing. "I know what position you'll be in, and it looks nothing like that." Both of the young men laughed.

"Come and have some wine, dear," Clive said, opening a bottle that he had retrieved before they went to walk the estate grounds. Blythdale's wine cellar was enormous. He used to play in it when he was a boy, and there were a number of secret compartments that he used to stash his private things.

He had selected a fine 1926 Chardonnay that came from a vineyard near his mother's family home.

"Oh, that's good," Charlie said, smacking his lips. "That's from the wine cellar?" he asked.

"Yes, but this is Clive's select stock, if you will."

"What does that mean?" Charlie asked seriously.

"It means it was my father's stock, until I selected it," Clive answered, bursting out laughing, while Charlie joined in.

After dinner, they got up and were leaving the dining hall, admiring the paintings of some of Clive's ancestors as they left.

"And what shall be our entertainment tonight, then?" Charlie asked, looking around the massive stone room, his voice slightly echoing off the rafters forty feet above his head. "Shall we read a play?"

"Oh, please, Charlie, we did that last night," Clive moaned. "Come here," he said sitting down on a love seat tucked into a grotto-like recession in the wall and patting the spot next to him. Charlie strolled over with a smile sitting down where Clive's handprint could still be seen on the seat's soft, wine-colored velour. The two kissed, and embraced.

"I know what entertainment I want tonight," Clive whispered into Charlie's ear.

"I imagine that means a reading of some sort is out of the question."

"You'd imagine correctly," Clive said, leaning over and kissing Charlie.

They made gentle love that night, but time was running too quickly for Charlie. Within four weeks he would be dead, leaving a grief-stricken Clive. Charlie would develop bronchial pneumonia, it would progress, and he would die. That was all there was to it, and nobody really saw it coming. Clive's grief, still weeks away, would be compounded by the fact that he would be unable to see Charlie at all for the final week, because Charlie's family had been told by the doctors that he was too sick and weak to see anyone except a few close relatives. Clive just wanted to see Charlie, and had no idea what the pneumonia was leading to, until he received a telegram from Charlie's mother, informing him of Charlie's death. It was the hardest farewell Clive never gave…

"Do you want me to drive? You're looking tired." It was

Claudette, breaking through his mind's sad thought.

"No, I'm fine," pushing his hand through his thick blond hair. "We'll be coming upon Béthune soon."

"Are you hungry?" She reached for a bag at her feet. "Madeleine packed us some food."

"Thanks, maybe later. I wish we had been given a rainy night for this trip. Nazis melt in the rain, you know."

"Oh, no, I hadn't heard that one," Claudette laughed, breaking some bread and bringing it up to her mouth, but her hand stopped mid-way between loaf and mouth because of what she saw through the slightly splattered windshield.

"This is odd, this is too soon," she said. It was a barricade. Not a guard post, like those going into the cities and larger towns, simply two, large, green army trucks pulled together at an angle in the middle of the road. Clive slowed their shabby, ridiculously oversized car to a halt, and waited as four men approached the car. Two were dressed in regular German Army uniforms, creaseless and pristine, their brass buttons ominously reflecting the headlights like the fiery eyes of wolves in the night. The third was dressed in a dark, SS officer's uniform, most likely an Ûntersturmfuher. The fourth was dressed in a relic of a French army uniform. They walked up to the car—the two conscripts walked to the back of the car and waited for orders, the other two took either side of the truck.

"Good evening monsieur," the French officer said, leaning in Clive's window. "Oh, and you too madam," he added, his eyes having gotten accustomed to the dark.

"Good evening," they replied.

"And where are we going tonight?" he asked. Clive noticed that he had a Parisian accent.

"We are going home," Clive said. "My new wife is coming with me back to Boulogne-Sur-Mer. The back of the car is loaded with my wife's belongings and some gifts."

"Well, then, congratulations," the Frenchman replied.

"Boulogne is such a lovely place, too, and to where I have been on a number of occasions. Might I ask, where are you coming from?"

"From, Arras, my hometown, and where we were married," Claudette piped in, handing the man their papers.

"Ah, Arras. I'm surprised you got out. They closed the city earlier. It would seem they discovered the bodies of two German soldiers, and they are now looking for two spies, an Englishman and a member of the French resistance."

"Shut up, you fool," the SS Ūntersturmfuher hissed over the roof of the car, standing at Claudette's window. "You give too much information away." His French was good, but it obviously came from a German.

"Oh, stop, captain. Don't you think I know an Englishman when I hear one? By his accent, this man was obviously raised in the South of France. Am I right monsieur, uh, Tanabre," he asked, looking at the documents again.

"I'm impressed," Clive said. "Yes, I'm originally from Montpellier."

"And, captain, does this lovely bride look like a member of the Resistance to you?" the Frenchman said, gesturing with his hands towards Claudette, who was thinking how thankful she was that she had chosen a homey, floral dress to wear for traveling.

"I have dealt with the Resistance, monsieur, and they come in all shapes and sizes," the Nazi said. "Nevertheless, we must search the car."

"As you wish, captain," the Frenchman replied. "Monsieur, madam, I will ask you to please step out of the car."

They opened their doors and got out. As they were getting out, the two lesser German guards were getting in the back. Clive and Claudette watched as they brought boxes and bags out of the car, opened them, and rummaged through them. They both held their breath when the box of books came out. The guard opened the box, lifted a few of the books, including the one with the rotor, and replaced them, folding the box closed again. Clive could feel his muscles relax. The French and Nazi officers stood next to Clive and Claudette in the tall grass on the side of the road. Clive took a chance on the Frenchman being so chatty.

"So, what is it you're looking for?" Clive ventured.

"We don't know, exactly," the Frenchman replied. "It supposedly looks a little like a small circular saw, the type that would cut wood in a shop."

"Again, you give far too much information away," the Nazi snapped. "I ask you to keep this information to yourself."

"I'm afraid for my husband and myself," Claudette jumped into the discussion. "English spies, Resistance members, two German soldiers murdered, are we safe traveling, monsieur captain," she said, turning with feigned concern to the Üntersturmfuher, and putting her hand delicately on his arm.

"Do not fear, madam," the SS officer said, his attitude now changed. "The incident was isolated, and you should not worry." He turned and shouted at the men to finish their search, and put everything back the way it was. As Clive and Claudette were bidding the officers a good evening, another car pulled up behind them, and the officers and two guards turned to go on their business of searching for the Englishman and the Resistance member. As they drove away, Clive's mind went to the description the French officer gave of the rotor, and concluded that a circular saw blade is exactly what the rotor looked like, minus the teeth, and was probably the best description of its appearance that he had heard.

They drove on in silence for about twenty minutes, the only noise was the grinding of the gears, and the struggling of the engine as the car moved up and down hills. Clive and Claudette were replaying the encounter in their minds trying to glean pieces of information they may have missed while talking with the French and German officers.

"I was thinking it might be quicker passing directly through Béthune," Clive finally said. "But, now I'm thinking that it would be safer to skirt the city, and go around it."

"I agree. I seem to recall a way we can take around Béthune that puts us where we want to be," she said, unfolding a map that she withdrew from her bag.

"What's more," Clive continued, "because it seems they are now on to us, we need to be careful with each step we take. If it all works out, in a few hours we'll be on the coast."

"I see how we can avoid Béthune," Claudette said, looking up from her map. "I'll let you know when to make the turn."

"Another thing to consider," Clive said, "is that that roadblock we just passed was in the middle of nowhere, and so we may run into others similarly placed."

They drove on through the French countryside, the silhouette of trees opening dark corridors for them to pass through. Claudette navigated them around Béthune, and they got lost only briefly, but recouped and were back on track in minutes. Nevertheless, they encountered no roadblocks, and for this they were grateful.

Clive thought about Roger, and even though they had only said good-bye the night before, he missed him. Distance played an interesting trick on time, he thought, so that the farther one is from the one they love, the more time seems to have passed since last seeing them. He was worried, because he didn't know what to expect from Roger when he got back. It's true that although Roger was mad, well, very mad, he did feel it necessary to come down to the wharf to see him off. Things would be all right, he thought. He knew enough about Roger by now to know that he couldn't carry a grudge for long, especially with him.

More interesting, Clive thought, was the idea of a long-term future with Roger. Certainly he had never met anyone like him before. Handsome, intelligent, loving and sweet, and yes, exciting in bed, too. Clive agreed that Roger and he were a wonderful team, and that they fit hand in glove. Neither was overly effeminate, which would help if they chose to live a life as roommates, where they could try to fit into society as confirmed bachelors. That would work, but they would never be able to stay in the same place for anymore than a few years. Some nosy-body would eventually put two-and-two together, that there had never been any comings and goings of young ladies, that the two seemed awfully close, *and what about all that thumping in the night*, a voice in Clive's head complained, and he smiled to himself.

"What's so funny," Claudette asked.

"Oh, I was just thinking about something that happened that was amusing—it would be hard to explain. I forgot how beautiful this part of France was, even at night, it's lovely."

"I've always loved it," Claudette replied, and both fell back into their silence. They had been traveling for some time now, and the traffic on the roads became very scarce, which happened around this time of the night. With the occupying forces around, not too many people liked to travel that late into the evening. Clive was surprised that they hadn't come across another roadblock, and was glad that he and Roger had carefully planned the return route. He was now more than ever worried about getting caught, because the Nazis seemed to have an idea of what they were looking for, and if one SS Officer decided they were too suspicious and brought them in for questioning, they would certainly miss the rendezvous.

They were crossing a bridge, about three hundred yards long, its metal girders sticking up on each side. They where halfway across the bridge when suddenly a brilliant light violated the darkness, coming from the lights of three cars parked at the other side of the bridge. It momentarily blinded Clive, who slammed on the brakes and brought the car to a stop about thirty yards away. The force threw boxes and bags down on them from the back of the car.

"Do you think we could run for it?" Claudette asked, looking over her shoulder through the back window, finally visible because all the boxes and bags had shifted.

"No, they have guns and would shoot us without thinking about it. And with three cars, they're bound to catch up with us.

Here they come." Several shadowy figures, eerily stretched and elongated by the headlights behind them, were walking towards them. The phantom things walked slowly, almost lumbering towards them in a patient, determined way.

"Well, this is it, Claudette," Clive said. "Let me thank you for all your help and hospitality these past two days."

"It was certainly my pleasure. Do you have any idea what they'll do with us?" she asked the figures now thirty feet away.

"Not the slightest." They both fell silent as the shadows moved in. Because the headlights were shining from behind the approaching figures, they remained in silhouette, and it was impossible to see anything about them as they approached the car.

"Your papers, please," a deep male voice demanded in native French through the driver's window. Another of the shadows flicked on a flashlight and directed it inside the car, directly in the faces of Claudette and Clive.

"No need for the papers, it's them," Clive heard a voice say. This was going to be hard, he thought, and in his head he apologized to Roger for not keeping his promise and making it back home.

"Claudette, my dear, you look like a fucking housewife," a voice said, bursting into laughter. It threw Clive off, and he thought his mind was playing jokes on him. But then Claudette responded with surprised laughter. "René Sinclair, you fool, you scared us half to death."

"We had to make sure it was you, mademoiselle, less we stop a pair of Nazi SS officers instead," another voice said from the dark.

"Quickly, we must move on," one of the voices said urgently. "Monsieur English, you follow us, eh?" The figures retreated hurriedly towards their cars. Clive put their own car into gear and drove after them. Within a few short seconds all four cars were speeding away.

"Um, I take it you know them," Clive jested.

"René is my cousin. He and I have been very close since childhood. Maybe we have been assigned protection for the rest of our trip."

"Would your people do that?"

"Well, I guess so, but I'm surprised they would risk several men for this. Maybe they've realized how important it is for the rotor to get back to your country." Clive looked towards her, and although he couldn't see her in the darkness, he knew her beautiful face was concerned. He had come to like this woman in the few short hours they had known each other, and he trusted and admired her.

"Claudette, there's something I have to tell you about the rotor…", he began, and for the next five minutes explained everything about the two teams being sent to France, and theirs being the decoy mission, that the rotor sitting hidden in the book was a fake. She listened and didn't interrupt or ask questions, but simply took it all in quietly. When he was finished, they drove for a few minutes in silence.

"I'm sorry I didn't tell you sooner," Clive finally said.

"Clive, my dear, do not worry about me," she said finally. "It was best that you didn't tell me earlier, because I don't know what I would have done differently. But, I have come to like you very much, and admire you for the fact that you would go through with the plan knowing that it was a fake rotor and a difficult mission. Now, more than ever, do I want to make sure you get home to England." Their hands met just above the stick shift, and they quietly held hands for a moment, until Clive had to shift gear. He returned both hands to the wheel, and they continued onward, following the three cars ahead to wherever it was they were going. Clive looked at his watch and was suddenly aware how close it was getting to the rendezvous time. *Wherever it is they're taking us,* he thought to himself, *it had better be close, nor take up too much more time.*

Loud and fast the four cars rounded a corner along the highway, illuminating the trees and shrubs along the side of the road, but only for a moment, and as quickly the area was awash in light, the night quickly reclaimed what was rightfully its own.

CHAPTER VI: SALVATION

The old man reached with spotted hand and pulled back the cuff of his raincoat. The move exposed the Rolex on his wrist, and a sad pain brought him back to the birthday his love had given it to him many years before. It was almost time to head back, he thought. He dreaded going.

It was one o'clock in the morning, and a second shift of staff had come in and relieved the previous group, which had been working feverishly to assist the return effort. Roger was grateful to have this small staff, and was amazed at how useful they were. If he, Alan, or Admiral Welles needed to find out the slightest piece of information, like the concentration of Nazi soldiers in a certain town that lay in Clive's possible path, one of the assistants would be given the question, and in a relatively short period of time, an answer would be returned. The map person was also most useful, and had set it up so that there were two pins that traversed the map, a black one, which marked an estimation of where Clive would be at that moment, and a white pin, which marked where he was last known to be. Roger was exhausted, but with the rendezvous scheduled to take place in three hours, he couldn't possibly sleep. The last two days felt like two weeks, and all he wanted was to get Clive back to England, go back to his apartment, and sleep with Clive wrapped in his arms.

"Are you asleep?" A whisper in his ear. It was Alan.

"No, just resting," Roger responded, raising his head and trying hard to focus on Alan's face.

"I'm sorry. You really do need to sleep, Roger."

"I know, I know. I promise I'll sleep when I hear he's on the ship and headed back. Right now, though, I don't think I can."

"They're after him, you know," Alan said seriously.

"Yes, I know. What's the news coming from France?"

"Well, from what we can tell, the Germans have certainly

found out that they had been mislead into staying clear of Arras. They're bloody well pissed off, and trying to catch up with him, and they know his route."

"So, this is actually worse than before," Roger said, hoping that Alan would disagree.

"Yes, it is. Because now the Germans seem to have a better grasp of the gravity of their situation. By now, they have probably guessed that we have more rotors than they thought we had, and they're terrified of the possibility of losing another to us."

"Do you think they'll make it?"

"I don't know, Roger. I'm sure the Nazis are reinforcing their shore points, and they're probably patrolling the waters more heavily along the coast. Luckily, this new craft can sit on the beach and wait, rather than risking detection out in the water."

"I see," was all Roger could say. He put his head on his folded arms, and once again tried not to fall asleep.

The car sped along, its gears noisily grinding, and its engine groaning to catch up with the three cars that hurried ahead. Clive wondered where they were going, and hoped they were aware that his rendezvous was in two hours, and that every minute not rushing to the rendezvous was time that would probably have to be made up.

"So, is your cousin a racecar driver?" Clive asked.

"No. He owns one of France's finest porcelain factories," she replied. "La Roselle Fine Porcelain," she said proudly.

"Is he from this area?"

"Yes, for most of his life." Claudette pushed back a box that had fallen on her shoulder. They drove for another five minutes, and finally pulled up in front of a tavern that was still open, and had one or two cars still parked in front. Claudette's cousin and another fellow approached Clive and Claudette.

"We don't have much time, cousin," René said, opening the

car door for her. He was forty, but already his hair was peppered with white, which was a nice contrast to his youthful face.

"René, what is this all about, will you be escorting us from here?"

"Not on your life. And you're lucky I don't pull you now and prevent you from going further."

"What do you mean?"

"From here to the English Channel, they are looking for you and your friend. But there's good reason. Come inside and I'll explain."

They entered the tavern, and Clive was surprised at how much cigarette smoke there was in the place, despite the fact that there were only seven men in the room. They walked through the tavern to a small back room that had a fireplace, some prints hanging on the walls, and a large round table in the middle with six chairs around it. Lit by an unadorned chandelier, the table was already set for five people, with some fruit and baked goods in baskets in the middle, which Clive was glad to see, because he was starving, and only realized it upon seeing the food.

"Claudette, this is my right hand man, Ilya," René said, putting his hand on the man's back. "He's from Moscow." They all shook hands, and sat at the table.

"René, what is this all about," Claudette asked.

"Simply put, my dear, your mission is a fake, it's not real. The rotor you think you have is fabricated. You see, captain, your government thought it would be best to have two teams come to France, one to get the rotor you need, and the other to act as a decoy. Unfortunately, my friend, you are the decoy."

"René, he knows all this, and he explained it to me," answered Claudette.

"But how do you know?" Clive asked him.

"That's the very reason why we're here. The Resistance, who has been in contact with your people in England, was instructed to change plans after the first team's failure to even reach France, which means they never would have been able to get the actual rotor that was waiting for them over in Corbie. I was instructed to get the real rotor, and try to intercept you, and believe me, it wasn't easy. We knew the path you were taking, but where to intercept you was difficult to select, and it greatly risked exposing ourselves to the Germans, because apparently they know the path you were taking, too."

"René, did my brother know about this decoy mission?" Claudette asked with grave seriousness.

"No, Claudette, Pierre knew nothing about it. He is now very upset with our command over the fact that they would place a resistance fighter in such danger without their knowing, and even more so that he had unknowingly sent his own sister into this mess."

"So, you're telling us that the first team didn't make it to France?" Clive asked.

"No, they didn't, their boat sank or something."

"And you have the real Rotor IV?"

"Yes, and we're to give it to you, and help you plan your new route back, because to tell you the truth captain, I'm really surprised you haven't been captured already. The entire path you were planning to take is swarming with Nazis."

"Where is the rotor now?" Clive asked.

"Well, monsieur, it's right in front of you," René said, spreading his arms wide across the table, but there was no rotor to be seen.

"I don't see anything," Claudette said. "René, don't play games."

René, ignoring her demand, smiled as he reached over for the plate that sat at the unused seat. "These fine China plates come from my factory, it is a new design and method I am using, do you like? We can make three dozen an hour."

"René," Claudette urged. "Where is the rotor?"

"My dear, calm down, it is right here." René held the plate up, and gave a circular gesture around its rim with his hand. "This is your rotor." And with careful grace, he slowly raised the plate upward, until it was directly under the bright light of the chandelier. Through the delicate thinness of the china, the light that passed through exposed a perfect silhouette of the rotor.

"Absolutely ingenious," Clive said.

"René, you baked the rotor inside that plate," Claudette said in amazement.

"It's what I do. When I see circles, I think of dishes and saucers, and so when we got the rotor in Corbie, putting it here made perfect sense. We're giving you the whole set, because I hear you've recently gotten married, Claudette, and so here's my wedding present to you. Now, while you eat, Ilya will show you the new route we've chosen for your safe return to Boulogne."

✿   ✿   ✿

Roger needed a cigarette, and so he and Alan were in the small courtyard they had found in the back of the cottage. It was a cold night, and the air felt invigorating and refreshing. Roger was almost finished with his cigarette when the cottage's back door opened and out lumbered Admiral Welles.

"Admiral, what are you doing out here?" Roger dropped the cigarette and stepped on it.

"I had to come out and tell you immediately. The captain has the rotor."

"What?"

"Sometime within the past two hours, Captain Westmore was intercepted by the French Resistance, and is now in possession of Rotor IV," the admiral clarified, reading it directly from the message that had been handed him not two minutes earlier.

"Wha-ho!" Alan shouted.

"The only problem is that the Germans are so hot on their

path, so to speak, that they are now returning to Boulogne on an undisclosed route. So, basically, until we pick him up at the rendezvous point, we won't know where he is."

"Admiral," Roger said quickly, "Captain Westmore and I have worked very hard together on this mission. Is there any way I might be able to stow myself on that ship picking him up? It would really mean a lot."

"Mr. Mathews, Roger, I'm sorry, but again, you are an American, and we can't jeopardize the involvement of your government. More to the point, if you remember what happened last night to the Alpha Team's ship, you would understand my concern in sending any ship over tonight, much less one with you on it."

"Yes, sir, I understand, thanks."

The three men followed the path of light from the cottage's door, back into the warmly lit command center.

✿   ✿   ✿

"Make your next right," Clive said, looking at a map that was being crumpled with one hand, while the other held onto a small flashlight. "That will put us on the D341, and from there, directly to Boulogne."

"What kind of directions did he give us?" Claudette asked, shifting gear and making the car buck. "This is too simple."

"I'm not going to complain. I'm still shocked, Claudette, at how things have turned out. I'm sure my partner is aware of what's happened, and I'm glad, because it's probably a major relief for him. He was very upset and concerned for my welfare when he found out that ours was a decoy mission."

"A loyal colleague is a good thing."

"Well, he's a bit more than a colleague, I'd say."

"A friend?"

"Maybe more than a friend, too," Clive dared.

"Ah, I see," Claudette said knowingly. "I know those friendships. For him to have been so concerned for your safety, he must really be a nice fellow, eh?"

"Amazingly nice. Here…" Clive said, reaching into a pocket inside his jacket and handing her the photo he kept there. "That's him," he said, shining the flashlight on it so she could see it and drive at the same time. "We had passed a portrait studio one day, and decided to go back and have our photo taken." Clive loved this picture, because it had been taken spur of the moment, with Clive in his naval uniform and Roger in a smart looking suit. They had taken a couple of posing shots, none of which he liked, but this one was perfect. It showed Roger sitting on a stool, with Clive standing next to him, one foot on the stool's crossbeam, his arm resting on bent knee as he leaned in towards Roger. The effect was that they looked as if they had been sharing a tender moment, but were interrupted by the camera. The photographer, who was exceedingly dainty, well understood what they wanted, and certainly delivered. The photo could well have been of two close friends during time of war, but for those with greater imagination and deeper understanding, they were two men in love.

"It's a wonderful photograph," Claudette said, her face smiling in the reflected glow of the flashlight as she handed it back to him. "You two are very lucky." Clive flicked off the flashlight, and the two drove on in silence.

It was quarter to two in the morning, and Roger was standing and staring at the wall map, trying to determine what alternate route it was that Clive was now following. The phones had not been used for some time because they had entered a blackout period. With such little information coming in, the staff was given the chance to eat, or catch up on well needed sleep. His eyes went to the large and simple clock that hung from a wire on the wall. Clive had only an hour and a half before the rendezvous ship would leave without him. By now, that very ship was probably already on its way across the channel, and would pace its crossing to arrive as close to the exact rendezvous time of three o'clock. Roger well understood that this was the time for things to get hairy, and his stomach began twisting in knots. But things had changed so much in the past twenty-four hours, who knew what the end would bring? Roger may indeed have Rotor IV, but now he also had three quarters of the German Army in France on his tail, which was an exaggeration, he was sure, but it may as well have been the case. Alan walked up beside Roger and looked up at the map.

"How many different routes could they have taken?" Alan asked.

"At least two, by my count."

"It's getting down to the wire, isn't it?"

"Yes. I want him home, Alan. What's the news from France?"

"We've intercepted several messages, but because the Germans know what's going on, all of the German Enigma machines have apparently been ordered to use the stricter naval code, and so we can't decipher them that quickly. It would be too late."

"The coast is probably swarming with Nazis," Roger admitted.

"True, but you know, Roger, you and Clive planned this thing well. You chose a rendezvous spot that didn't have a watch post for a mile or two in either direction, and it's in pretty shallow waters, which helps. So, if the Germans, when they erected their sentry points along the coast, found it was that lacking in the need for protection, it's possible that maybe they still do, and have added only a nominal amount of fortification."

"I would like to think that, Alan. I really would." The two men fell silent, and stood looking up at the map like schoolboys looking at a blackboard whose contents neither understood.

"We're doing well," Clive shouted over the grinding gears. "It's now two-thirty, and we'll be there within ten minutes." They had stopped earlier to relieve themselves on some deserted country road, and Clive had picked up the driving from there.

"We are ahead of schedule, then," Claudette said. "That's good."

"True, but I don't trust schedules anymore. Too many changes have been made to this mission. I'm not going to trust anything until I'm on that boat heading back."

"What will you do when you get back to England?"

"I don't know. After this, I don't think I will accept any more missions. However, I'm too young to retire from the navy, and I couldn't anyway with the war still on. So, I'll probably be commissioned to some ship or other—serve out the rest of the war, and then go on to teach at university. That is, if Oxford still wants me."

"They'd be a fool not to have you." She smiled, and put her hand on his forearm for a moment, then let it slide back to her lap.

"We'll be there shortly, by the looks of it, and we haven't run into any roadblocks," Clive said.

"We're on the D-940 roadway, which runs along the shore, so we can go down any of these roads here," Claudette said, gesturing to occasional roads on the left. Actually, they weren't roads as much as they were dirt paths that meandered dangerously down the steep cliffs to the beach below.

As the car turned a sharp curve in the road, the inside of their car burst into light, and once again they found themselves staring into headlights. This time, there were four vehicles, and they were blocking the road completely.

"Shit," Clive said.

"All we can do is tell them the same story," Claudette uttered. "We just got married and are returning home."

"I'm afraid they've heard that too many times today,

Claudette."

Clive slowed and stopped the car. He pulled out his pistol and slid it between the seats in a well that was somewhat hidden.

"Get out of the car please with your hands up," a voice bellowed from behind the headlights. Clive and Claudette opened their doors and slid out of the car, their arms extended upwards. All of a sudden a German soldier approached with a gun pointed at them, and two other soldiers came up behind them and frisked them, confirming Clive's decision to play it safe and hide the gun in the car.

"You can put your arms down now," one of the soldiers said. When the soldiers stepped back, a car door slammed, and three figures moved towards them and walked into the lighted area. The leading figure was an SS Sturmbannfuhrer, which was the equivalent to a major, Clive recalled. The headlights reflected on the patent leather brim of his hat, a design that forced the eye to fall on the emblem of the eagle and swastika that sat above the brim. Although he had a calm smile, his face was lit from below, giving it an evil and ominous look. He was wearing a long, mouse-colored coat, which he had just finished removing, exposing his decorated uniform with Maltese crosses and merit pins. The two men behind him were Rottenfuhrers, or privates.

"Well, Captain Westmore, we seem to have finally found you," the approaching man said. "I am Sturmbannfuhrer Klaus Von Schletter of the Fuhrer's tenth division, and you are under arrest."

"What are you talking about?" Claudette said. "This is my husband, Stephan Tanabre, and we are..." but Clive cut her off.

"Don't even bother, Claudette. Alright then Major Von Schletter, you have us, but unfortunately we do not have what you are looking for."

"Not true, we know you have the Rotor IV. Now where is it?"

"We don't have it, it was a fake, and so we didn't take it."

"Don't toy with me, captain, where is the rotor?"

"I told you, we don't have it."

"Search the car," Von Schletter ordered, his eyes still on Clive. "Leave nothing unopened, nothing unsearched."

Clive and Claudette were pushed to sitting positions on the ground, with a soldier standing over each of them. They watched as the soldiers started taking boxes and bags out of the car. They did it orderly, with two in the car handing things out to the others, who would open a box, search its contents, and then place the box or bag in a pile to the side. They made it so close that Clive could hear the waves crashing on the beach in the distance. Now they were helpless, and all Clive and Claudette could do was watch as the Nazis continued to search each bag, box, and parcel.

Roger looked at the clock, it was a little after three in the morning, and he was wondering what was going on at the other side of the Channel. Was Clive already on the landing ship and on his way back? Was he still rushing to get to the rendezvous point? They wouldn't know until the landing ship was close enough to the English coast to radio a message. What would he do if Clive hadn't made it? Would it mean he was captured, or just delayed and missed the rendezvous? There were so many questions. It was the eleventh hour, and everything would now unfold.

"Well, this is it," Alan said, coming up behind him. "The rendezvous is taking place, and Clive will be back in a couple of hours."

"You seem so sure."

"I like to remain positive until I know otherwise. But I have a feeling that when the ship leaves in twenty minutes, Clive will be on it."

"God, I hope you're right," Roger said, as the clock made a tick as the minute hand advanced a notch.

Clive watched as the box of plates was lifted out of the car. One of the soldier opened it, and started lifting the plates out one by one and handing them to the other. They got to the bottom and, satisfied that they had searched the box, started putting the plates back. Clive drew a breath of relief and let it out slowly. They may have been captured, but he was damned if he was going to give the Germans the satisfaction of capturing the rotor. He counted the plates as they were being handed back and placed in the box two at a time—one and two, three and four, five and six, seven and then it happened, Clive watched in horror as the two plates slipped from the hands of the soldier and fell to the ground shattering into fragments. It took Clive only a second to see the rim of the rotor sticking out from the pile of shards.

"You fools," Von Schletter yelled in German walking over to them. "I told you to be careful with…" and then he stopped, his mouth still open. In the time it takes for an idea to come, resolve itself, and go, something happened in Clive's head. It was an explosion of epiphany whose salience stopped all other thoughts in their tracks. So, Clive was determined to play his last and only card.

As Von Schletter started bending down to pick up the rotor, Clive shouted "No!" and heaved himself upright and started running towards Von Schletter and the rotor. It was on his third step that he heard the gun go off, and he immediately fell to the ground. It took only a second for the searing, white-hot pain from his leg to reach his brain. "Clive," he heard Claudette scream behind him as he fell, his cheek pressed to the ground, small clouds of dried dirt rising near his nostrils as he breathed. He closed his eyes and waited for the next bullet to find a more vital target. It took only a second before he heard the second discharge. He gasped, and waited for the end. He heard Claudette scream once more.

"In the name of the Fuhrer, hold your fire," a voice loudly shouted. Through his agony, Clive saw four new SS Officers standing on the periphery of the lighted area of headlights. His eyes immediately fell on the officer who stood in front of the other three. It was obviously someone of the rank of Oberfuhrer, one of the higher SS ranks. His long thick trench coat was open, exposing a dark green uniform underneath, which acted as a superb canvass for the military accoutrements that adorned it. His hat was similar to Von Schletter's, but along with other medals and pins, he had a second Maltese cross that hung from his chest pocket. On each lapel were two lightning bolts that reflected the light of the headlights like actual bursts from the sky. His face was cold and stern, the mouth hinted of cruelty. Behind him, and standing at attention, were three very rugged-looking privates, first class by the look of it, their right sleeves each held an armband that proclaimed "Deutschland."

Clive mostly noticed the soldier whose gun was pointed to the sky, and who stood next to the ominous Oberfuhrer. He was a strikingly good-looking second lieutenant, whose mouse-gray uniform suggested a powerful body underneath. It was this Untersturmfuhrer who had just fired the second shot. Despite his agony, Clive's mind wondered how three such handsome men could be grouped together by chance. The Oberfuhrer walked further into the light towards Von Schletter, who offered a loud and earnest "Heil Hitler."

"Heil Hitler," the Oberfuhrer offered nonchalantly. "Sturmbannfuhrer Von Schletter, I am Oberfuhrer Karl Strauss. We have been following your superb handling of apprehending these spies. Their smuggling of top-secret information has been spoiled by your efforts, and you are to be commended. Your work, I assure you, will be rewarded." He said this while walking to where Von Schletter stood. He stopped with his feet almost in the pile of shards, clapped his gloved hands twice, as gently as one would clap at the ballet, and immediately one of the lesser SS Officers quickly walked over, picked up the rotor, and handed it to him. Despite his poor German, Clive was following this exchange and understood enough of what was being said to easily fill in the blanks. He could now see Strauss's face more clearly, and it looked vaguely familiar. Actually, it looked very familiar, and Clive started thinking of which previous mission he could have seen this SS officer.

"However," Strauss continued, sliding the rotor into his coat's oversized pocket and withdrawing a cigarette case in the same move, "it is now time for these spies be transferred to the Gestapo, and taken directly to Berlin." Strauss quickly inserted a cigarette into the holder that he withdrew from his other pocket.

"But Oberfuhrer Strauss," Von Schletter dared with mock deference, "My orders were to take the spies prisoner, and transport them to army headquarters in Paris."

"You dare question me?" Strauss said coldly, striking a match and lighting the cigarette. "Well, then, let's be sure, Herr Von Schletter, shall we? Let's call Major General Frichstein, who personally gave me my orders, and make sure we have our stories straight. I'm sure he won't mind being awakened at quarter past three in the morning for clarification on an order he had already given!"

Strauss nodded to one of his men, who went to the parked cars. While he waited, he took another drag from his cigarette, and slowly let the smoke out in a large cloud that drifted away like an apparition. The moment lasted as Von Schletter looked to his men, down to the injured Clive, and back to Strauss. Clive was in enormous pain, but followed every second of what was happening. He watched the uncertain Von Schletter standing above him, not sure what to do. He saw Strauss looming above him as well, waiting for Von Schletter to make a decision. Clive watched as Strauss's eyes narrowed whenever he took a drag from his cigarette—oh, yes, Clive had seen this face before, but still couldn't remember from where. He was not one to forget a person, and his level of recognition led him to believe he had seen it more than once, and rather recently. His attention was diverted to the soldier who had gone to the cars, and was now returning with a portable phone-radio, which he held out in front of him like an offering.

"Please, Sturmbannfuhrer Von Schletter, be my guest," Strauss said, beckoning with his arm to the phone. It took Von Schletter only another moment to acquiesce.

"Perhaps I have been to rash, Herr Oberfuhrer," he said, trying to maintain some pride by bowing his head theatrically. "What will you do with them, may I ask?"

"We will transport them to Berlin, interrogate them, and maybe put them on trial. Normally, I'd shoot them myself here on the spot, but there are apparent political currents involved, and so they are to be spared, at least for the time being." Clive was glad that Claudette didn't speak German. He looked over at her and she looked upset, but she was keeping quiet. Strauss clapped his gloved hands again, and gestured down towards Clive. Immediately one of the officers came over with a small bag, while the one with the phone returned to the car. The handsome soldier went to one knee and roughly tied a tourniquet around Clive's leg just above the wound, Clive screamed in pain, which seared through his leg and into his torso. If he had been anywhere else, he probably would have lost consciousness, but circumstances prevented that. One of Strauss's other soldiers appeared, and the two lifted him up. The third walked over to Claudette, and pulled her struggling to her feet.

"So, Von Schletter," Strauss said, dropping his cigarette and stepping on it. "I will make sure that Gruppenfuhrer Frichstein is made fully aware of your full cooperation in this matter."

"Thank you, Herr Oberfuhrer. Heil Hitler!"

"Heil Hitler," Strauss said with a lame salute. He turned and walked towards the cars followed by his men and their two prisoners.

"Schnell, schnell," Strauss hissed to his men under his breath, and the small grouped hurried faster. Clive's pain had turned into a fiery throb, but he was alert. They made it to a large black limousine, and Clive noticed through his pain the swastika flags that adorned the front. He felt himself tossed into the back, and a wave of agony flushed through his leg. He felt Claudette reach over to support his injured limb. The two privates jumped in the front, and Strauss and his right hand soldier slid in the seat across from Clive and Claudette.

Clive was now scared for the first time that maybe this was, in fact, the end. They were to be transported to Berlin, and who knew what would happen to them from there. He was surprised that Claudette, as a member of the French Resistance, hadn't already been shot at point blank. He leaned over towards her.

"Claudette, are you all right," he asked quietly.

"Shhhh, I'm fine," she responded, still gently supporting his leg. He rested his head against the door and his mind went back to worrying. He'd never see Roger again. He'd never make it to England. His mind was a whirlwind of defeat and despair. However, someone speaking loudly, but calmly suddenly interrupted his thoughts.

"Smith, you'd better get us to the rendezvous fucking-ass quick, do you understand me?"

Clive's mind must have been playing tricks, he thought, because the words he heard shouted were not only in pure English, but also with an American accent. A small light was turned on in the back, faintly illuminating the back seat.

"Yes, sir!" came the military-style shout from the driver, and this time again in English with an American accent. Clive was dumbfounded for only a moment, and then, his mind putting the last piece to the puzzle, suddenly remembered how he knew Oberfuhrer Strauss.

"Agent Pomboi!" Clive turned and declared loudly, his leg throbbing with each syllable. It was the American FBI agent who Roger couldn't stand, and who had been so stoic and self-possessed whenever they had met with Admiral Welles. His mind quickly recalled Roger's urgings that Pomboi had an accent, and now Clive understood why.

"We meet again, Captain Westmore," Pomboi said. "I'm sorry about your leg, but you really shouldn't have made a run for the rotor. How do you feel?"

"I'll live, but I am totally confused." He felt as if he were dreaming now, because nothing like this could ever happen in real life.

"Clive, you know these men?" Claudette asked in French, unsure of what was happening.

"I'm here to make sure you get to that landing ship," Pomboi said matter of factly. "We're actually only about a quarter of a mile away, and looking at my watch, we have ten minutes to spare."

"But how did you…I can't believe that you were able to…"

"Captain, don't underestimate American Intelligence and the FBI. We may not be in the war, but we're pretty certain it will come soon enough, and so we're preparing as best as we can for that time. That is why we knew it was essential for you to make it back with the rotor. And that is why when the plans changed, I volunteered to come and make sure you made it out successfully. Actually, I've been following you since you left Arras. Like yourself, this is not my first time behind enemy lines…ah, here we are." The car began descending at a steep angle, and after a minute, leveled itself out as it rolled onto the soft sand and stopped. The sound of crashing waves could be heard in the dark.

"Let's go see if we can find your rendezvous party," Pomboi said, and the young Americans in the front jumped out of the car and opened both doors. Pomboi stepped out, followed by his handsome first officer. The three leaned back in to help the wounded Clive, more gently this time. Claudette followed, the interior light warmly lit her face, and it registered a little surprise when one of the soldiers offered a supporting hand as she stepped out of the car.

"But what about Claudette?" Clive stopped and asked, realizing he couldn't just leave without making sure she was safe. "What is to be done for her? She's been instrumental at every step I've taken here."

"Mademoiselle Du Mont's return has already been arranged," Pomboi said, taking out a cigarette and lighting it. "We have the car, more swastikas than a German Youth march, and the uniforms. What more do we need for a pleasant, uninterrupted ride to back to Arras? Don't worry, she be safely returned home. Now quickly, let's go." Clive was carried by two of the soldiers and Claudette followed. They made it down do the water, and Pomboi's first officer pointed a flashlight down the beach and flashed a signal—they watched but there was no reply. He tried the same signal once more, and again there was no reply.

"Turn and signal down the other way," Pomboi ordered through his teeth. The officer complied, and the flashes illuminated the foamy tops of cresting waves. Clive held his breath, and suddenly, from a couple hundred feet down the beach, the shaft of light from a small flashlight signaled back.

"Well, Captain. There's your landing party, and they'll be here in a minute or two to get you—we must be off. Come mademoiselle, we must hurry to get you back to Arras." Claudette looked at Clive, who was now sitting on the beach, his leg, with its blood soaked tourniquet, resting on the sand. She quickly went down to him on her knees.

"Clive, I will miss you." She was almost crying.

"I'll miss you, too, Claudette. You go back and take care of Madeleine. When this thing is over, I'll come and find you, all right?" She leaned in and kissed him on the cheek. She looked at him for one more moment, and then got up and started following the soldiers. Clive's leather bag kicked up some sand as it landed next to him on the beach. "The rotor's in the side pocket," Agent Pomboi said with the cigarette dangling from his lips. "Congratulations on a successful mission, captain." Pomboi turned to follow his men, then stopped and looked at Clive.

"Oh, and captain, give my best to your friend," he said, taking a drag from his cigarette. "You two make a good team."

"Thank you," Clive responded, wondering if he knew. Clive watched Pomboi's cigarette bounce away in the night, finally fading into the dark. A few minutes later two dark figures came up the beach. They found him, alone and lying on the beach with his leg shattered to pieces. But he was alive, and he had the rotor.

✿   ✿   ✿

The command center was quiet, and all attention was directed to Alan, whose luck it was to answer the call when it came in from the radio operator. His hand was still frozen in mid air with the wave that had seconds before silenced the room. "Yes…I see…that's wonderful…yes…hold on one moment, please." He pulled the receiver away from his ear and covered the mouthpiece with his hand. Turning to the quiet room, he noticed that all eyes were trained on him. Roger and Admiral Welles were standing near the large map.

"Captain Westmore is on the ship, and they're just a few miles out. And yes, he does have Rotor IV!" Alan said smiling. Everyone broke out cheering and clapping, and Alan glanced over to see a beaming Roger looking back at him with a smile that was, for the first time in days, honest, sincere, and overjoyed. "Hold on a second, everyone." Alan said, putting the phone back to his ear and telling the radio operator at the other end to continue. Alan listened, but suddenly grew serious and concerned. "How bad is it," he asked into the phone. "Yes, we'll arrange that immediately… and please radio that back to the ship…Thank you." He turned back to the silent room. "However, he's been shot, and is in immediate need of medical attention. They're asking that an ambulance be there to meet them when they dock."

It took only a second for Admiral Welles to point to one of the assistants and order them to arrange the ambulance. He turned and told his personal assistant to have his car brought around. Alan and Roger were already standing solemnly by the door waiting for him.

"Come on, gents," the admiral said lightly as he passed them to the door. "The ship will be in soon, and we need to get down there to meet it."

It took them twenty minutes to get to the docks, and although the earth was still dark, the sky was just beginning to brighten to the point where one could make out the silhouette of the trees as they pulled in. Roger noticed that the ambulance was already there, a military truck painted white with a large red cross on its side. The driver, doctor, and a nurse were standing next to it and talking. Their car pulled to a stop in front of the harbormaster's house. It took only a moment for the short, stocky man to emerge and great them. He was dressed in greasy overalls, and was wiping his hands on a rag that seem to have less grease than the man's clothes.

"Admiral, good morning," the harbormaster said in a deep English accent—it was all Roger could do to understand him. "They should be docking in about ten minutes."

"Thank you, harbormaster," the admiral replied. "You seem to have your hands full there."

"Yes, sir. One of 'em vessels came in 'ere last night with a chipped prop, and I'm fix'n it for 'em."

"Why isn't the ship's chief engineer fixing it?" the admiral asked.

"Well, yer see, sir, the men of this ship have been a'working forty-nine hours straight, admiral sir, and the man who should be doing this is getting the sleep he wonts 'n deserves." The harbormaster blinked innocently and looked up at the admiral, who was standing, obviously moved.

"Gentlemen," the admiral finally said, turning to Roger and Alan, and putting his hand on the old man's shoulder. "This is England, and this is why we'll win this war." Roger and Alan nodded, and the harbormaster smiled back at the three men, not fully understanding why he seemed to be getting such recognition.

"Has there been any more word on Captain Westmore's injuries?" Roger finally asked.

"No. The cap'n has been shot in the leg, and when our wireless operator was last a'speaking with the ship, he was tended for by the first mate, he was. I thinks, sir, that even though he needs a doctor right fast, he'll be well in the long run."

By the time the ship rounded the harbor and came into sight, the sky was brilliant with colors. Roger watched it sailing towards the pier with the warm knowledge that Clive was on it. Maybe he was injured, but he was alive, and somewhere on that wonderful landing ship that was fast approaching. His eyes strained to make out the figures on the ship, and finally recognized Clive's beautiful blonde hair. He was being supported by a crewman, and was draped with a thick flannel blanket. It was obvious that he should have been inside, but Roger knew that Clive had probably wanted to go up on deck as the ship entered port. Now only a hundred yards out, Roger watched as Clive finally saw him, pointed at him, and then waved. Roger waved back, and his heart ached in relief. Clive had made it home.

The ship docked and the crew began tying the vessel down, but before the gangplank could even be lowered, Roger wasted no time in asking the ship's captain, who was standing on the deck in front of him, for permission to come aboard. The captain gave him a smile and a welcoming gesture. Roger jumped the three feet onto the deck and quickly made his way to Clive, who was now sitting with the first mate kneeling next to him. He had over-exerted himself, and Roger could see the blood soaked pants and tourniquet. Clive looked very pale, and had probably lost a lot of blood.

"Clive, what did you do to yourself?"

"Oh, I decided to take a German bullet in the leg," he said with a faint smile. "You should try it someday."

"Stop, we need to get you help," Roger said, standing up and rushing to the rail of the ship. "Get that doctor and nurse up here, NOW!" he shouted to no one in particular, and went back to Clive.

"Stop worrying, I'll be fine," Clive said weakly. "Don't get your panties in a bunch," he added, knowing that Roger hated when he used that expression. The young sailor next to them looked perplexed.

"The doctor's coming now, Clive. You don't know how happy I am you're back."

"Yes, I do, because it must be about as happy as I am to be back. Hello, Mr. Mathews," Clive said looking into Roger's eyes.

"Hello, Captain Westmore," Roger replied, and the two smiled at each other. Soon, the clanging of feet on the metal stairs brought the Admiral, Alan, and the doctor and nurse. The ship's captain and crew came to look, too.

"Admiral," Clive said looking up at the towering Welles. "I believe this now belongs to His Majesty's Government." He held up the small leather bag that contained the rotor.

"Good work, Captain Westmore. Good work, indeed. Please, everyone, stand clear for the doctor."

The doctor stepped forward, and all watched and listened as he looked at the bandage, and asked Clive a few questions.

"He needs surgery, of course, and we need to get him to the hospital right away," the doctor finally said to everyone. Like a fallen Roman general, Clive was placed on a stretcher, and everyone seemed to want a hand in carrying it safely to the waiting ambulance. When they got there, the landing ship's captain and crew wished Clive a speedy recovery, and returned to their vessel.

"Admiral Welles," Clive said as he was about to be hoisted into the ambulance.

"Yes, Captain."

"Permission to debrief my partner prior to my formal debriefing to you and others," he asked, not looking at the admiral, but instead at Roger.

"Permission granted, Captain Westmore," the admiral said with a nod. "Nurse, as this is a top-secret matter, you'll need to ride up with the driver and doctor."

"If we need anything, we'll bang for you," Roger said,

jumping in alongside the stretcher that now rested in the back of the ambulance.

"We'll see you at the hospital," Roger said to the Admiral and Alan, who had been standing by, quietly enjoying the reunion. He leaned over from where he was sitting across from Clive and closed the ambulance's door.

With the drapes in the back windows of the ambulance closed, they had enough privacy for Roger to feel comfortable taking Clive's hand.

"Clive, are you okay? Are you in any pain?"

"I'm alright, and the doctor just gave me a shot of morphine."

"We've been trying to follow your every step for the past twenty-four hours. You came back, you made it back to me."

"I told you I would. You were in my thoughts every step of the way. The doctor said the bullet barely missed my femur, and that although bad, it's only a flesh wound. So, I should be out of the hospital just in time."

"Just in time for what," Roger asked.

"In time for our holiday to the Lake District. I put in for the leave time two weeks ago, and already have our rooms reserved at this perfect little inn that I'm sure you are going to love" Clive smiled. "I knew we would need to get away, just the two of us."

"You are unbelievable," Roger's smiled, but then grew serious.

"What's the matter?"

"What happens after the vacation? What do we do then?"

"I was thinking that while we're on vacation, we might discuss, well, consolidating our lives. I don't know what the future holds, Roger, but there's one thing I do know, and that is that I can't imagine my life without you in it." Neither man spoke for a moment.

"I love you," Roger said softly, pulling Clive's hand to his lips and kissing it.

"I love you, too," Clive turned his hand so it rested on Roger's face. Just then they heard the muffled sound of one of the amublance's front doors close, and the vehicle slowly lurched and rocked as it moved forward.

The sun was blazing, and it looked as if this early March day would bring a warm dry air. The ambulance slowly pulled out of the dockyard through the crowd of people coming to work. As they stepped aside to let it pass, it left in its wake a gap that was soon filled again with the crisscrossing paths of sailors and longshoremen reporting for the day's duty, because their jobs needed to be worked, their tasks to be completed, their war to be won.

The old man walked to the precipice, and looked down at the inviting rocks below, the waves crashing upon them and retreating back into the foamy ocean. From this height, even the gulls that swooped and sailed over the water looked like small white dots. His mind played out hundreds of events that had happened to him since the end of the war, when they moved here and set up their lives in a perfect little way. But perfection was dead, and nothing could ever bring him back. He stood looking down into the water until he felt the housemaid walk up from behind him. She gave him a minute to get used to her presence before she spoke

"Monsieur, you must come back now, it is time for the funeral," she said softly.

"I'm coming, Claudette," he replied tiredly, "I'm coming."

ABOUT THE AUTHOR

DAVID JUHREN opened his first book when he was five years old, and fell in love with reading. When David came out of the closet in his early forties, he put his new prospectives and energies to use, and wrote his first novel, *The Code*, and is currently working on number two, along with various short stories.

Juhren is the Executive Director of The LOFT, the Lesbian, Gay, Bisexual, and Transgender Community Center. The Center serves the LGBT community of New York's Lower Hudson Valley.

He lives with his partner, Michael, in Westchester County New York, where he is joined on weekends by his two fabulous kids. You can visit AM on the internet at:

http://davidjuhren.blogspot.com

THE TREVOR PROJECT

The Trevor Project operates the only nationwide, around-the-clock crisis and suicide prevention helpline for lesbian, gay, bisexual, transgender and questioning youth. Every day, The Trevor Project saves lives though its free and confidential helpline, its website and its educational services. If you or a friend are feeling lost or alone call The Trevor Helpline. If you or a friend are feeling lost, alone, confused or in crisis, please call The Trevor Helpline. You'll be able to speak confidentially with a trained counselor 24/7.

The Trevor Helpline: 866-488-7386

On the Web: http://www.thetrevorproject.org/

THE GAY MEN'S DOMESTIC VIOLENCE PROJECT

Founded in 1994, The Gay Men's Domestic Violence Project is a grassroots, non-profit organization founded by a gay male survivor of domestic violence and developed through the strength, contributions and participation of the community. The Gay Men's Domestic Violence Project supports victims and survivors through education, advocacy and direct services. Understanding that the serious public health issue of domestic violence is not gender specific, we serve men in relationships with men, regardless of how they identify, and stand ready to assist them in navigating through abusive relationships.

GMDVP Helpline: 800.832.1901

On the Web: http://gmdvp.org/

THE GAY & LESBIAN ALLIANCE AGAINST DEFAMATION / GLAAD EN ESPAÑOL

The Gay & Lesbian Alliance Against Defamation (GLAAD) is dedicated to promoting and ensuring fair, accurate and inclusive representation of people and events in the media as a means of eliminating homophobia and discrimination based on gender identity and sexual orientation.

On the Web: http://www.glaad.org/

GLAAD en español:

http://www.glaad.org/espanol/bienvenido.php

SERVICEMEMBERS LEGAL DEFENSE NETWORK

Servicemembers Legal Defense Network is a nonpartisan, nonprofit, legal services, watchdog and policy organization dedicated to ending discrimination against and harassment of military personnel affected by "Don't Ask, Don't Tell" (DADT). The SLDN provides free, confidential legal services to all those impacted by DADT and related discrimination. Since 1993, its inhouse legal team has responded to more than 9,000 requests for assistance. In Congress, it leads the fight to repeal DADT and replace it with a law that ensures equal treatment for every servicemember, regardless of sexual orientation. In the courts, it works to challenge the constitutionality of DADT.

SLDN
PO Box 65301
Washington DC 20035-5301
On the Web: http://sldn.org/

Call: (202) 328-3244
or (202) 328-FAIR
e-mail: sldn@sldn.org

THE GLBT NATIONAL HELP CENTER

The GLBT National Help Center is a nonprofit, tax-exempt organization that is dedicated to meeting the needs of the gay, lesbian, bisexual and transgender community and those questioning their sexual orientation and gender identity. It is an outgrowth of the Gay & Lesbian National Hotline, which began in 1996 and now is a primary program of The GLBT National Help Center. It offers several different programs including two national hotlines that help members of the GLBT community talk about the important issues that they are facing in their lives. It helps end the isolation that many people feel, by providing a safe environment on the phone or via the internet to discuss issues that people can't talk about anywhere else. The GLBT National Help Center also helps other organizations build the infrastructure they need to provide strong support to our community at the local level.

National Hotline: 1-888-THE-GLNH (1-888-843-4564)
National Youth Talkline 1-800-246-PRIDE (1-800-246-7743)
On the Web: http://www.glnh.org/
e-mail: info@glbtnationalhelpcenter.org

Lightning Source UK Ltd.
Milton Keynes UK
21 March 2011
169613UK00001B/66/P